WHISPERS IN THE DARK

CHRIS MCDONALD

ERIKA PIPER BOOK 2

RED DOG
UK

Published by RED DOG PRESS 2020

First Edition

Hardback ISBN 978-1-913331-38-2

Paperback ISBN 978-1-913331-23-8

Ebook ISBN 978-1-913331-24-5

www.reddogpress.co.uk

To my Blood Brothers, Rob and Sean.
Here is to friendship, laughter and happy memories made during a
very strange time.

PRAISE FOR WHISPERS IN THE DARK

"Chris McDonald is one of the great emerging UK crime writers and *Whispers in the Dark* demonstrates why. Dark and compelling from page one, it's one of the standout mysteries of 2020."
— **M.W. Craven**, author of *The Puppet Show*

"Cements McDonald's place as one of the UK's brightest stars in crime fiction. The second book in the DI Erika Piper series follows on with such panache, compulsion and humanity that you can't help but be gleefully consumed by it. Emotionally wrought with a frightening, unpredictable mystery at its core, *Whispers in the Dark* pulls the strands of all-too-real fears tight and binds them fast with whip-smart plotting, sharp characterisation and prose you can't turn away from. McDonald proves once again that he is not just one to watch, but a brightly emerging star of UK crime fiction."
— **Rob Parker**, author of *Far from the Tree*

"Wow! Chris McDonald has written a book that will make your heart and head spin. His observations of people are sensitively and accurately drawn, and his descriptive style so good that you feel present within the world he has created. Erika Piper is the sort of woman I would love to go for a drink with and definitely would want her on my side in a crisis."
— **S.E. Moorhead**, author of *Witness X*

'Drags you down to some dark depths, with real heart-in-mouth moments, leaving you every bit as emotionally rag-dolled as the characters. DI Erika Piper is a great addition to the crime fiction family, and deserves a place on everyone's reading pile."
— **Robert Scragg**, author of *All that is Buried*

... and we never saw eye to eye,
To see past those lies,
When did I die?
Because I'm not alive...

An excerpt from the suicide note of Manon Marchand

THEN

THE BOY WAS in his usual spot, cowering in the claustrophobic space between the sideboard and the wall. The well-worn carpet in the living room was even more threadbare here, such was his reliance on this little slice of solace. The peeling wallpaper licked at the small of his naked back. During happier days, when he had used this secluded corner for games of hide-and-seek, the feeling had elicited a little giggle that had given him away. Today, however, the paper felt more like a witch's finger clawing at his back.

He could hear his mother and father in the kitchen. The door was closed, so he struggled to make out their words, but from their tone, it sounded like they were having another argument. The boy peeked out over the top of the furniture that currently concealed him, and stared at the front door. He considered making a run for it. If he could just get outside, he would be safe, at least for a while, at least until his father's anger had abated somewhat.

Just as he summoned the required level of courage to make his escape, the kitchen door flew open with such force that it almost separated from its hinges, crashing into the living room wall. His father lurched in, glugging from a bottle of whiskey. He lifted the bottle to and from his mouth with such gusto that more of the amber liquid drenched his beard and dropped to the carpet than actually entered his mouth.

His grubby white vest, stretched over a muscular body, was stained with dirt and what the boy supposed must be blood. The boy didn't know what job his father did, but he knew it was dangerous, as his mother would often sob when he was gone and, more than once, unsavoury characters had appeared on the doorstep. This was often followed by raised voices and violence which spilled out onto the street.

The boy's father set his bottle down on a table and stood with his hands on his hips, facing his son. His unfocused eyes rested on the boy and a look of disgust formed on his face.

'Get the fuck out of there,' he slurred, and a small amount of urine escaped the boy, soaking the front of his shorts. When the boy didn't move, his father repeated his order, louder this time.

The boy crept from his hiding position and stood facing his father, who was already undoing his belt. The squeak of the leather filled the otherwise silent room. He could feel his hands trembling, so he intertwined his fingers behind his back. His father didn't like it when he showed weakness.

'Heard a story about you today, boy,' his father sneered. The boy knew better than to reply, so instead, he let the remark linger. His father made a point of removing the belt slowly, dragging it through each loop.

'Heard you were stealing,' he eventually elaborated. He reached into his pocket and pulled out a packet of cigarettes and a lighter. He set the unopened cigarettes on the same table as the bottle of whiskey. With a click of a button, flames leapt from the top of the lighter. His father simply held it in front of him for a while, his eyes fixed, seemingly lost in the hypnotising flickers of light. The boy knew better than to let his guard down.

'Do we steal?' his father asked, still somewhat subdued.

'Dad, I...' the boy started. His father simply held up a hand, stopping the boy mid-explanation. With the other hand, he brought the lighter down onto the boy's exposed chest. The red-hot metal melted into his pale skin and, as the boy's screams filled the house, his father's smile widened.

After what felt like an eternity, his father relented, pulling the lighter away. The boy stared in horror at the vicious welt that was rising near his nipple and prayed to a God that he did not believe in that that would be the end of his punishment. Sadly, the silent prayer fell on unlistening ears.

His father reached out and pinched the nerve in the nape of the boy's neck, forcing him to his knees. A noise akin to a cat's hiss filled the room as his father slowly unzipped his jeans and slid his underpants to the floor. In that moment, the boy hated everyone. He hated his father, the man who should be his rock and sworn protector. He hated his mother, the woman who should do anything for her child but who was no doubt trembling at the kitchen table, turning a blind eye to this torture. Most of all, he hated himself. He hated the fact that he was too weak to stand up to his evil father and too scared to tell anyone about what happened behind closed doors.

As his father advanced towards him, he vowed, there and then, that when he grew up, he would have his revenge. The things he would go on to do would make his father's actions seem almost reasonable.

NOW

1

AS THE OPENING notes of Mr Brightside ring out through the marquee, I know that the three-course meal nestled uncomfortably in my stomach will not be classed as a good enough reason to resist the dancefloor I'd so far done a good job at avoiding.

'Erika,' Tom says to me, 'it's time to dance.' He tips his head back and finishes the rest of his pint. Then, ignoring my protestations, grabs my hand and leads me into the middle of the crowd. A horde of acquaintances and strangers suddenly become as inseparable as lifelong friends as we dance and sing along to the anthemic rock song.

Middle aged women hold imaginary cigarettes to their mouths whilst a group of Liam's rugby teammates run their hands over each other's chests. Tom pulls me close as the song comes to a climax and kisses me on the lips, the taste of beer registering on my tongue. As a more modern song I am unfamiliar with begins, I ignore his pleas to remain on the dancefloor and make my way back to my seat, where my handbag has remained unattended. I pull out my phone and thankfully there are no notifications. Relieved, I cram it back into my bag and look around at the merriment.

The marquee has been elegantly decorated. Fairy lights hang from the ceiling—miniature stars against an ethereal backdrop. Once full, now slightly deflated pastel-coloured balloons bob around in the middle of circular tables, alerting the guests to their table number. The tables fill one half of the marquee, whilst the other half is dedicated to the black-and-white tiled dancefloor.

4

A small stage at the front is currently playing host to the function band, led by a singer who looks a little like Ryan Gosling and who appears to be appreciating the attention from any women present.

At the centre of the crowded dancefloor is my partner, Detective Sergeant Liam Sutton, gazing into the eyes of the man who became his husband just a few hours ago, apparently oblivious to anyone else in the room.

The song ends amid a cacophony of cheering and as the band announce that they are having a short break, Tom returns to the table, plonking himself rather heavily on the chair beside me. He throws his arm around my neck and nuzzles his sweaty forehead into the side of my face.

'Erika, I reckon you could have a drink now,' he slurs. 'It's nearly the end of the night and he hasn't called. I imagine you're off the hook.'

I pull my phone out and check again, the screen still clear of any attempted communication. As most of my team are here at Liam's wedding, DCI Bob Lovatt, my boss, has asked me to be on call. He promised to try and get through the day without me, but wanted me to be contactable in case of emergency. I deliberate on Tom's offer but decide to decline, not wanting to risk Bob's fury if I am needed.

As Tom makes his way to the bar, almost stumbling into the red post-box being used as a Polaroid picture depository, I grab the foil packaging from my hand-bag and slip it into the pocket of my dress before pushing myself out of my seat and leaving the marquee. The tight feeling that I've had in my chest for the past few months feels especially restrictive tonight. I make my way up the steps and into the luxurious hotel, the grounds of which are currently playing host to the erected marquee.

I reach the toilets and find that all five cubicles are occupied, so I lean against the wall and watch two women squinting into the mirror, giggling about the good-looking lead singer and attempting to reapply their make-up drunkenly. The taller of the two glances towards me and a flicker of recognition spreads across her face.

'I told you she'd be here,' she screeches suddenly, shocking the woman beside her, and causing her to smear lipstick up her cheek. She swears at her friend for surprising her, though the first woman doesn't seem to notice. The one who recognises me sets her make-up brush on the sink and staggers over to me, enveloping me in a sweaty hug.

'Liam said you'd be here. I'm Eileen,' she says in my ear. 'You caught that bastard who killed that actress… Emma…'

'Anna,' I correct her as I wiggle out of the hug and take a step back, re-establishing my personal space. Just before Christmas last year, I'd enjoyed fifteen minutes of fame, having been part of the team that had apprehended a murderer who had become worldwide news, on account of killing three people, including the famous actress Anna Symons. The attention, thankfully, had subsided reasonably quickly, but every so often, I still noticed members of the public raking me over with a knowing stare.

I'd even been interviewed about the case by a petty criminal, from the back seat of the police car on our way back to the station. He told me his mates won't believe him that he was arrested by THE Erika Piper, and asked could he have a picture to prove it. I'd impolitely declined.

'Anna, that's it,' Eileen replies, holding herself up against the wall and pointing at me. 'You're the one that caught him. I loved her films so much.'

She loses her balance and slides down the wall, balancing on her knees. The alcohol and the occasion seem to be getting the better of her, and it looks like she is about to have a little drunk-cry. Her friend, angry a few seconds ago, sets her lipstick down.

'Come on, Eileen,' she coos, whilst trying to lift her friend to a standing position. I smile, her words reminding me of the one song Liam point-blank refused to have played at his wedding.

One of the cubicle doors swings open and I make my excuses, nodding at Eileen as she makes me promise to find her downstairs so that she can buy me a drink to say thank you. I close the toilet seat and sit down, slipping the foil packet out of my pocket. I twirl it around in my hands and run a finger over the name of the tablets; paroxetine, trying to decide if what I am about to do is the best course of action. Tom would be annoyed if he found out I was taking more than the recommended dosage. As would Bob and Liam. And my dad. But they don't know how it feels. They don't know the struggle that has been raging within me for the past six months. They don't know how much energy it takes to force myself out of bed and put on a brave face.

I could talk about it, of course. A number of people close to me have offered. DCI Bob even floated the idea of more therapy, paid for by the police, though quickly relented having gauged my reaction. I did have one round of therapy, and definitely felt the benefit of it, but I am worried about the stigma attached—the hushed voices of my colleagues who don't need to spill their guts to a trained professional in order to do the job they're paid to do.

I run my finger over the glossy scar on my cheek, an everlasting reminder left by The Blood Ice Killer, the serial killer we'd managed to bring to justice at the end of last year, on the night he was finally caught, and my mind flashes back to the shard of glass being dragged slowly across my skin. I can feel the goose bumps spring up over my body and a cold film of sweat forms on my forehead.

Mind made up, I push one of the tablets out of its little bubble and pop it into my mouth. It's small enough to take without a drink, though I do feel it sticking slightly as it makes its way down my throat. I sit for a few more minutes with my head in my hands, gathering my thoughts, before unlocking the door and making my way back towards the party.

I stop at the top of the steps that lead back to the garden and gaze out at the scene below. Stars twinkle in the inky night sky and a full moon acts as a beacon, illuminating the immaculate hotel grounds. The gravel paths, lit by Victorian style lampposts, frame the lush green lawns upon which the marquee currently resides. Carefully maintained ivy travels up the facade of the impressive seventeenth century building. It's all so perfect, yet I feel so disconnected from it all.

I start my descent towards the marquee, taking care not to totter over in the unfamiliar high heels. The noise spilling out of the open flap tells me that the band have reconvened and are enjoying the adulation of the drunken crowd once more.

I paint a smile on and re-enter, the heat of the room hitting me like a slap in the face. I join Tom—who now has his cravat tied around his head—on the dancefloor for the remainder of Livin' On A Prayer, before remembering that I hadn't taken my phone to the toilet with me. I slink off the dancefloor towards the table, unzip my bag and grab my phone. My heart sinks as the illuminated screen shows two missed calls from DCI Bob.

Cursing the criminals of Manchester and hoping that he is simply calling to tell me to stand down, I sneak out of the marquee again and return his call. He answers on the first ring.

'Caught you on the dancefloor, have I?' he says. There is no hint of joviality in his voice. In fact, he sounds sad.

'Do you need me?' I ask.

'I do,' he confirms. 'I would've tried to get by without you, but it's bad.'

Before hanging up, I ask him to text me the address of where I am needed and assure him that I will leave right away. The gravel crunches underfoot as I make my back into the marquee. Tom is now slumped on his seat and stares at me with faraway eyes, barely registering that I am saying goodbye. He hugs me like a child and, as I gather my belongings, assures me that he will behave himself. I kiss the top of his head and make my way through the crowd towards Liam.

Liam, unlike Tom, has resisted using his garments to make himself look like a ninja. Ever the fashionista, his paisley tie and fitted shirt remain as crisp as they were at the start of the ceremony nearly ten hours ago. With his shaved head and angular jawline, he could have been just as much of a hit on the catwalks of New York as on the streets of Manchester. Still, fashion's loss is Greater Manchester Police's gain.

As I approach, he registers my expression and his wide smile becomes a disappointed frown. He throws his arms around me and mumbles something in my ear, though I can't make it out over the din of the music. His stubble rubbing against my skin is ticklish so I pull away and give him a kiss on the cheek, before bidding him and his husband, Dylan, farewell and leaving the party for good, my mind already focussing on what I am about to encounter just a short drive away.

2

HAPPY TO BE free of the uncomfortable heels and back into my trusty work shoes, I push the pedal to the floor and accelerate down the mostly empty main road towards the east of the city. Headlights from the car behind shine brightly, though it indicates and turns into a side street seconds after I tilt my rear-view mirror.

After a couple of minutes, I turn left at a rather gothic looking church. Uplights cast a sinister glow across the dark stone walls, and a cross with Jesus attached to it above the tall wooden doors throws out an ominous greeting.

I turn onto a long residential street filled with terraced houses which stretch into the darkness and out of sight. The red brick two up, two down style houses are identical, except for one which is currently sticking out like a sore thumb, thanks to the police presence outside.

The blue flashing lights of the stationed police cars are a far cry from the pulsating lights that are probably still illuminating the dancefloor of the marquee I've just left. The wedding party may only be a few miles down the road but, as I bring my car to a stop a little further up the street, it feels like a world away.

I step out of the car and start towards the house currently being guarded by a harried looking police officer. I have to push through a boisterous group of youths, some with clothing pulled over their faces. This may be to combat the rapidly dropping temperature or, more likely, to conceal their appearance from us. This is gang territory, after all.

I duck under the police tape and give the young officer's shoulder a reassuring squeeze, noticing he looks even more stressed up close. I sign the log book, checking my watch and realising that it has just passed midnight, before slipping a protective suit over my clothes and stepping into the house.

The small area between the door and the hallway is home to several pairs of trainers, neatly stacked in a wooden shoe rack, and a few brightly coloured coats and hoodies, hung up on a row of hooks. A security chain dangling from the door jangles in the wind, and I notice that there are a number of locks acting as further security measures on the back of the door.

Martin, head technician of the Scene of Crime Officers, is in the living room, barking orders at his team. He is a squat, studious man with ever roving eyes that never miss a beat. The bulldog breed. When I walk into the room, he greets me with an almost imperceptible raise of his hand.

'Anything doing?' I ask him, gazing around the orderly looking living room. A cheap leather sofa rests against one wall, grooves from a recent occupant still present in the material. Controllers for a games console have been set tidily on a bookshelf, and a huge wall-mounted flat screen television fills the space above the fireplace.

Garish wallpaper with purple and silver flowers stretching towards the ceiling covers one of the walls. The other three walls are painted a dull mauve. It lends the room a rather dark, oppressive feel. The air is musty; an ashtray with cigarette butts propels the scent of marijuana around the enclosed space. The temptation to open a window is overwhelming, though I know I mustn't, for fear of losing a modicum of evidence.

'Aside from a small amount of cocaine and weed, not much,' he answers, pointing to a little cabinet at the side of the sofa. I imagine that, since there is a keyhole and no key, that one of the SOCOs have worked their lock-picking magic on it. 'It could be for personal use, but we think he might have been a dealer. Though, if he was, he was small time. At least, he wasn't known to the police.' He raises his hand and points to the ceiling.

'All the action is up there.'

I tell him to let me know if he comes across anything of note, before leaving the room and ascending the narrow staircase. The steps are steep and with no banister to hold onto, the climb feels precarious. There is a scrum of SOCOs at the top of the stairs, so I wait until they have finished their conversation and have begun to make their way down, before edging around them. The small hallway has three doors leading off it. One of the doors is slightly ajar and I can just make out a grotty toilet in the darkness.

From inside the room straight in front of me, I can hear my boss' low rumbling voice. When I enter, he has his back to me and is deep in conversation with another man. The room is sparsely decorated. A double bed has just about been squeezed in and a narrow, pine wardrobe has been shoved into the corner of the room. One of the doors is missing and the sleeves of a number of checked shirts protrude through the gap. The maroon walls are bare, no art or framed photographs, nothing to offer a clue as to who the room belongs to. The only telltale sign of any foul play is the spray of blood on the wall opposite the end of the bed.

'This had better be good. You know how much I love to dance,' I say. As DCI Bob turns to face me, I notice that his eyes are bloodshot and his face is ruddy; tear tracks glisten on his cheeks. My laugh catches in my throat and my smile rapidly disappears.

'He was my best friend,' he mutters. 'I should've done more.'

The man standing next to Bob puts his hand tentatively on his shoulder. 'There's nothing anyone could've done. You know that. Go home. Erika will deal with this one.' Bob shakes the man's hand and gives me a vacant smile, before wordlessly leaving the room.

The man in question is John Kirrane, the best forensic pathologist in Manchester. John had played his part in apprehending Anna's killer half a year ago, and I was pleased to see he had been on call tonight. Of course, seeing John was not usually something I hoped for, charming as his company was, as it typically meant there was a dead body in the vicinity.

'What was all that about?' I ask him. He simply steps to the side, and it's only then I notice the two bodies at the foot of the bed, lying in an enormous pool of blood. One man is lying face down on the floor, his arms stretched straight above his head. His legs have been obscured from view from where the other body has fallen—that of an older man.

John and I take a few steps closer to the bodies and only then, when I see what remains of the older man's face, do I realise why Bob was so upset. He's one of us. DCI Clive Burston was well known throughout the Manchester area. He was a brave man who had helped solve some of the toughest cases the city had thrown at him during his time as a DI. He and Bob rose through the ranks together and became DCIs at roughly the same time; Bob had stayed in Manchester and Clive had moved to Bolton, though he still came back for social occasions with the old guard.

Like Bob, he can't have been far off retiring. How had he ended up here, dead, in the bedroom of a squalid council house in the east of Manchester?

'Bob was just telling me that Clive had been on gardening leave for the past month. Apparently, he had botched a case at work. Misplaced some evidence. Someone who was going down for a long time walked free because of it.'

I exhale a sympathetic sigh and take a step back in order to survey the scene in front of me. Clive is dressed in casual clothes; a black shirt, tan chinos and a pair of leather boating shoes on his feet. He has socks on, of course. The old fellas don't subscribe to the shoes, no socks look, and rightfully so. His outfit suggests he was not here on official police business. Currently, being on a forced leave of absence would lend further credence to that idea. *So what other reason could possibly lead him here?* Whatever it was, it's cost him his life.

I bend down to examine his body, noting that the only apparent injuries are to his head, which is currently resting against the wall, his neck bent at an odd angle to the rest of his body. There is a single hole in the side of his head. His face shows no sign of an exit wound, meaning the bullet that caused the damage must be lodged in his brain. Or what's left of it. This is a positive—a bleak positive if there is such a thing, as we may be able to match the bullet to a gun, possibly helping us in our search for the murder weapon, which I've been told is not present in the room.

John calls down the stairs for the crime scene photographer and after making sure that Martin has finished combing the room, we roll Clive's body over on to the stained, cream carpet and spend a few minutes taking it in. As suspected, his torso and legs are untouched. Only his face shows signs of violence. A yawning gash just above his right eyebrow is weeping blood, and a deep purple bruise is beginning to form under his eyes and around his nose. The photographer snaps the body from many different angles, both up close and personal and from a distance.

'Do you think the killer did this?' I ask John, indicating the battered face.

He bends down and moves his pocket torch over the facial injuries, causing eerie shadows to be cast on the walls. He then stands up again and surveys the room.

'Yes, but indirectly,' he answers. 'I think he was shot in the head from the doorway. As he fell forward,' John mimics the act of toppling forward from a spot in the room near the door, 'I think he hit his face on the bed frame and then came to rest where we found him.'

I get up off my knees and examine the wooden bed frame. At the end of the bed, on the sharp corner of the cheap plywood, is some deep crimson liquid. I give John a little smile.

'God, you're good,' I whisper, which elicits a laugh. 'So, the positioning of the entry wound and the way he fell would suggest that either he didn't get to see his killer due to the speed of the attack, or that they conversed and Clive simply accepted his fate.'

'It's a pretty clean shot,' notes John. 'Makes me think that he knew what was coming. If you thought you might be about to be shot in the head, you'd duck and dive, wouldn't you? You'd do anything to get out of the way. The angle of the wound and the fact that the killer has only had to fire once, suggests that Clive stood like a statue and let it happen.'

I mull over what John has said and, despite not knowing the man personally, decide that he wouldn't have done that. Every human being in the world, when faced with their own mortality, has a fight-or-flight reflex, and as a police officer, you are trained to recognise threats in every situation. I'd bet my life on the fact that Clive would not have stood still, knowing that he was about to die. Unless… There must be another reason.

With Clive's cause of death more or less confirmed, we move on to our second victim. Now that Clive's body has been moved, it is clear to see the injuries the man lying face down on the carpet has sustained. His skin tight, white T-shirt and grey tracksuit bottoms have been stained a vibrant red. Four bullet wounds punctuate his back, like a fragmented exclamation mark; the broken skin still oozing blood. Red rings snake around his outstretched wrists, indicating that at some stage of the evening, he had been tied up. I notice that he is not wearing any shoes, which may suggest that he is the occupant of the house and was simply settling in for a quiet night.

My mind whirrs with possibilities and I wonder if these two very different men had arranged to meet here for a sexual encounter. The fact they have been found in the bedroom, and one has evidence of being bound, helps the theory carry some weight. I voice my thoughts on the matter and John nods sagely. He tells me all will become clear during the post-mortem.

As with Clive, we turn this body over and perform a quick assessment, though the hard yards will be completed later in the mortuary. Aside from the bullet wounds, no further damage has been caused to the young man. No bruising, no cuts or scrapes, no sign of a fight.

Something isn't right here.

'Do we know his name?' I ask.

'Not yet,' John replies.

'Do you know who called it in?'

'I do,' John answers. 'He is in the kitchen waiting for you.'

I leave John to organise the removal of the bodies to the mortuary and make my way down the stairs, through the living room and into the kitchen. Dirty plates and plastic ready meal cartons with mouldy sauce in the bottom of them litter the worktops. The small fridge beside the washing machine gives off a loud buzzing noise, which I imagine would become very annoying if here for any length of time.

Leaning against the back door, under the supervision of a uniformed police officer, is a young man. On first glance, he appears to be roughly the same age as the unnamed victim upstairs. His hood has been pulled up over his dark, closely cropped hair and, as I approach, he attempts to focus on me with bleary eyes. When he speaks, I realise he is drunk.

'You gorra help me,' he slurs, before I can even introduce myself. Tears begin to drip down his face and he makes no effort to wipe them away.

'How can I do that?' I ask him.

He suddenly looks frantic. He makes an attempt to come towards me, though the uniformed officer takes a quick step in his direction, forcing the young man to come to a halt. Looking at me with pleading eyes, he whispers.

'I know who did this to Marcus and I think he's coming for me next.'

3

THE CLOCK ON the table in the interview room shows that it is just after half-past nine in the morning. Usually, the room is a time-free zone; just one of the ploys used to create a psychological advantage over the interviewee. Today, however, there is no need for such psychological warfare.

The young man opposite me, Daniel Price, has spent the night in a police cell at his own insistence. Considering what he had seen and the state he was in last night, I felt like it was probably the right call.

This morning, he looks younger. The effects of the alcohol have worn off, though he seems to be nursing a hangover. His eyelids are slightly droopy and what we can see of his eyeballs are bloodshot. Despite spending the night in the cells, and not having access to a razor, his chubby, boyish face is lacking any hair. As he sits across the table from me, I can't help but think that he looks like a lost boy whose mother is late picking him up from school.

He reaches out, lifts a plastic cup filled with water and takes a small sip, before setting it down again. His eyes have remained focused on the same spot on the table since he sat down a few minutes ago.

When I speak, his eyes drift up to meet mine. He looks scared. I explain to him that we are going to record our conversation and that he doesn't have to answer anything that he doesn't want to. I end with a reassuring smile and he gives me a little nod in return. I press the green button on the console and a matching light begins to glow, letting me know that the recording has begun.

'Detective Inspector Erika Piper, commencing interview with Daniel Price. Interview conducted at—' I glance at the clock in front of me, '—09:37 on Sunday the fourth of August 2019. Daniel has declined the offer of legal representation. He is here of his own free will.'

I let him have a minute to take in what is happening, before asking my first question.

'Tell me a little about yourself.'

He snaps his neck up and looks at me with wide eyes.

'I thought this was about Marcus,' he says.

I tell him that it is about the whole situation and whether he likes it or not, he is now part of it. I then repeat the question.

'My name is Dan. Daniel Price. I am 20 years old. I have lived on the same street as Marcus all of my life. We've been best friends since we were in primary school. We were both in Miss Baxter's class in reception. I remember being really scared and he came up and asked if I wanted to play in the sandpit with him. We've been joined at the hip since.'

Tears start to pool in the corner of his eyes, the realisation setting in that he has lost his best friend of nearly two decades. I press on, trying to keep him on track.

'Were you the one who discovered the bodies?'

'Yes,' he says.

'And what time was that?'

He takes a few moments to think. 'I think it was just before eleven o'clock. Marcus had said he'd come and meet us for a few beers down at the pub, but he never showed. I assumed maybe he'd gone to see Kylie instead.'

'Kylie?' I interrupt.

'His bird. But as I was walking home—past his house—I saw his door was hanging open. He's quite security conscious, so I went in to see if he was okay. There was no sign of him downstairs so I went up to the bedroom… and…'

'And what can you tell me about Marcus?' I ask, keen to keep him in a positive frame of mind.

The corners of his mouth upturn, no doubt remembering the good times they'd spent together over the years.

'Marcus is a dude,' he says. 'He'd do anything for you, for anyone. We grew up together. His mum and dad got divorced when we were little, then mine did when we were teenagers. We helped each other through the hard times. He's funny, good with the ladies, generous with his money…' He trails off. Whether he's aware of his persistent use of the present tense or not is unclear. I don't bother correcting him.

'What did he do for work?' I ask.

The question wipes the smile off his face.

'No comment,' he mutters, looking anywhere but my direction.

'Was he a drug dealer?' I ask, no longer requiring a verbal answer as Daniel's expression has just confirmed my suspicions.

'He'd only started,' he starts, panicked, his voice wavering. 'Another friend of ours offered him an opportunity to make quick cash, and he jumped at the chance. I tried to warn him off it. We've lived in the area long enough to see the shit drugs cause. I pleaded with him not to be part of the problem, but he promised me that it was a short-term thing and then he'd be out. He said he was just helping a friend.'

The temperature in the room has increased a few degrees and as Daniel takes his hoodie off, his T-shirt rides up his torso, exposing a blue and red triangular tattoo on his ribcage. He realises a nanosecond after I spot it and pulls the material back down, covering his body. It's a tattoo that I am familiar with.

'You're part of the Bennett Street Rebels,' I state.

He grimaces.

'Was Marcus?'

'We both were,' he nods. 'Living on our street, you can't avoid joining. I know the gang has caused some issues over the years,' he says, almost apologetically, 'but I try to keep my involvement to a minimum.'

'Is this who Marcus was dealing for?'

He nods again.

'You said last night you knew who did this. Can you tell me?'

He exhales a long breath. 'About a week ago, when Marcus and me were in his gaff playing FIFA, we heard the back door open. He usually keeps it locked; like I said before, he's very conscious of his security, especially after being given the drugs he was gonna sell. He must've forgotten to re-lock it after taking the bins out that day or something. Anyway, Olly Pilkington, you know him?' he asks me.

I confirm that I do. Oliver Pilkington is the leader of one of the most notorious gangs in Manchester—the Longsight Lunatics. Oliver, or Olly as he prefers to be called, has risen up the ranks and has been leader now for about two years. He is violent, devious and cunning as a fox. Many departments of the Greater Manchester Police, including my own, have had run-ins with Oliver Pilkington over the years and though he has thrown many of his own gang members under the bus to save his own skin, no-one has been able to find enough evidence to bring him down, yet.

'Well, Olly Pilkington is standing in the kitchen, casually leaning against the side like it's his place and we are the ones invading. He pours himself a cup of water from the tap and grabs a knife from the drawer. Then he comes and sits on the sofa beside us. He still hasn't said a word yet. I considered running for it, but assumed he'd have some of his cronies blocking the exits. Anyway, as he's spinning the knife in his hand, he accuses Marcus of coming into his area and dealing to his customers. I can tell Marcus is shitting himself. He apologises and says that if he did, it was a mistake that won't happen again. Olly seems to accept it. He sets the cup down on the floor, stands up and offers Marcus his hand. Marcus stands up too, and, as they shake hands, Olly plunges the tip of the knife into Marcus' forearm. He tells him that he can make mistakes too, and that the next time he does, it'll be a big one. He then pulls the knife out of his arm, goes into the kitchen, wipes the blood off it with some kitchen roll, pockets the knife and casually strolls out of the back door again, slamming it as he leaves. Now I'm worried that he's going to come for me next.'

I tell him that we will keep a police presence outside his house for the next few nights, which seems to reassure him. I also give him my card and make him promise me that if he feels nervous or threatened, to give me a ring.

As we exit the interview room and head towards the waiting room, I suggest to him that as a seemingly articulate and sensible young man, he might consider moving away from the area, perhaps to complete a university course, in order to escape the clutch of the gang. He laughs at the mention of university and tells me that no-one from his area has ever gone on to university. I want to ruffle his hair and hurl inspirational quotes at him.

Dream big.

Be the change you want to see.

But I don't say any of this. I don't want to seem uncool.

As he sits down, I assure him that we will do everything in our power to keep him safe, and to catch Marcus' killer. He thanks me and pulls out a pair of headphones, shoving the end of the cable into his phone. It seems I have been dismissed.

I exit the station and head to the police car park. I check my watch and realise I'm running slightly late for my meeting with John Kirrane. I pick up the pace slightly, but stop in my tracks as I round the corner and realise there is someone unexpected leaning on the bonnet of my car.

'What are you doing here?' I ask, confused.

4

DETECTIVE SERGEANT LIAM Sutton smiles at my confused expression as he slides off the car, tucking the back of his shirt into his trousers. Even though the day is not overly sunny, oversized Ray Ban style sunglasses sit on the bridge of his nose, no doubt in an attempt to shield sensitive eyes.

'I can't afford to give you a head start on the case, can I? You'll be insufferable,' he laughs.

'Isn't your husband annoyed that you are abandoning him the day after your wedding?' I ask.

'Nah,' he says, shaking his head, 'he drank far more than me and will be hanging today, so he'll be no use to anyone. In fact, he'll probably be glad of the peace and quiet! Also, we're not going on honeymoon until October, so I need to work as much as I can to afford the trip. Japan is quite expensive apparently.'

I remember him telling me all about his honeymoon on the way back from arresting a man involved in a burglary in the north of the city. The plan is to fly to Japan to watch England play three matches in the Rugby World Cup. When my limited knowledge and interest in the sport failed to initiate the kind of conversation Liam would've hoped for, our felon in the back had leapt to my rescue, discussing who they thought would be best at full back, which I assumed was a position on the field, and the might of 'our' scrum compared to 'theirs.'

'I'm glad you're here,' I tell him. 'I'm just about to head to the hospital, it's autopsy time.'

He pulls a face and opens the car door, sitting down gingerly in the passenger seat. I hide a smile as I slip into the car beside him, before starting the engine and indicating left out of the car park towards Manchester Royal Infirmary.

JILL, THE RECEPTIONIST, sets two polystyrene cups of coffee on her desk and informs us that John is running a little behind schedule, but that he should be with us shortly. The car journey to the hospital had been used to discuss yesterday's wedding, which already seems like a lifetime ago.

Apparently, after I left, his brother had fallen over on the dance floor. The rugby lads had assumed it was on purpose and initiated a pile on of epic proportions. There'd also been a conga line and the traditional dance off.

I lift the coffees off the desk and walk over to the chairs outside the mortuary, where Liam is attempting to get comfortable. I use the delay to fill him in on the case so far; the two bodies, the young man who found the dead and the shadowy presence of Olly Pilkington.

'So, it's gang related?' he asks.

I hold my hands out, palms upward. At this stage, it's hard to know. It certainly appears gang related, but my many years in the job have taught me to never accept the obvious.

The door to the mortuary opens and John Kirrane emerges. He greets us and tells us to go in and get into our suits, while he nips to the toilet. Liam and I get up from our seats and walk into the room. The stench of chemicals attacks my nose and I immediately feel my eyes water as they try to flush out any foreign bodies. I accept a translucent overall from his assistant, Trevor, and pull it on, just as John darts back in through the door, stepping into his mortuary boots.

John leads us over to a metal gurney, where a white sheet has been laid over the waiting body. He pulls it away to reveal the long, thin, mostly hairless body of DCI Clive Burston. He moves over to

23

the console and starts the recording device, immediately beginning to narrate his examination of the body.

I stare intently at the face, as that appears to be the only part on the front of the body that has sustained any damage. The bruising from smashing his head off the bed frame has intensified and spread. Despite the discolouration of his skin, he looks at peace. Once John is happy that nothing has been missed, he tilts Clive's head slightly to the right, to get a better look at the entry wound of the bullet. He measures it and instructs Trevor to photograph it. As he picks up the mechanical saw to begin the more invasive part of the autopsy, Liam turns a particularly ghastly shade of grey and makes his way, at pace, to the exit. John smirks.

'What's wrong with him?' he asks. 'He's usually got the stomach of a bull.'

'He got married yesterday, so he's a bit worse for wear,' I explain.

'Why the fuck is he at work today?' he explodes. 'He should be confined to bed, eating cherries off his husband's—'

'Ah, should we get back on track?' I interrupt, pointing to the microphone hanging from the ceiling. The sound of the saw whirring into motion answers my question.

Trevor makes a small incision in the back of the head, before John uses the saw to cut through the bone and free the brain. With great care, he removes the organ and sets it gently on the worktop. It's clear, even to me, that that the bullet has caused a significant amount of damage, and after a small amount of dissection, John confirms that the .22 bullet lodged in his grey matter is indeed what killed him. Clive's body is left to the team to be fixed up, ready for burial, as Marcus' body is wheeled out of the fridge and into the main room.

Marcus' frame is lean and muscular. The definition in his arms and torso show that he clearly enjoyed going to the gym. On his arm is a vivid red cut in the process of becoming a scar. His head has recently been shaved and parts of his scalp are completely bare, suffering from what looks like alopecia. Perhaps he kept it shaved close to the scalp to try and hide the hairless parts. On his left pec is the same gang tattoo that adorned Daniel's midriff.

John repeats the same routine on this body as he did on the last, and decides that he probably would've survived three of the bullets, had the fourth not punctured a chamber of his heart. The redness around his wrists has subsided, but markings consistent with those made by rope are left behind. We again discuss the possibility that the two men were meeting for a sexual encounter. John debunks the notion of anything physical having occurred by performing a few checks on the body, but theorises that perhaps one of them got cold feet upon meeting and this led to the violence.

'If Marcus did wimp out of a bit of how's your father and Clive fired the gun at him before turning it on himself, the weapon would be there, wouldn't it? Maybe Marcus's girl came into the room at the wrong time and saw something she didn't want to. From what I understand, it was the type of house that might well've had a gun lying around.'

I make a note to discuss this line of questioning with Marcus's lover when we meet.

Having been subjected to a rigorous examination, Marcus's body too is left in the care of the assistants, whilst I follow John to his office.

'Have you spoken to the families yet?' he asks, as he logs onto the computer on his cluttered desk.

'Not yet, though we are on our way to Bury now to inform Clive's wife, and then we're heading over to Marcus' girlfriend's house. She seems to be all he had. Daniel told me that both his parents died a few years ago.'

'Do me a favour. Can you ask Clive's widow if he was left-handed?'

I throw him a look. 'Do you have a theory?'

'More of a hunch than a theory,' he replies. 'and I don't want my hunch to lead your investigation. But find that out for me and things might become clearer.'

I tell him I will, thank him for his work and leave the room. Liam is sitting with his head in his hands, sweating.

'I knew I should've said no to the tequila,' he mumbles, sheepishly. He gets to his feet and we walk, him rather gingerly, towards the door. As we step outside into the warm sun, a strange churning begins in my stomach. It can't be from alcohol, as I didn't have any, so I put it down as sympathy pain for my partner.

5

THE JOURNEY TO Bury takes us past Heaton Park and up the M66. It doesn't take very long. Usually, we'd spend driving time listening to anthems from the seventies and eighties; ABBA being particular favourites, but today Liam and I put on our professional hats, turn the radio down and use the time wisely; discussing the information garnered from the autopsies and firing theories at each other concerning the actual murders.

We keep reeling off the same questions—*what was Clive doing there? What is the link between the Detective Chief Inspector and the juvenile drug dealer? How could they possibly have known each other?* Yet we are no closer to an answer as we enter Clive's street in the attractive area of Greenmount in the north of the town.

Six expensive looking homes are nestled in the cul-de-sac. They are similar in style; red brick, bay windows, though with different coloured doors. The double driveways house an impressive array of cars and perfectly manicured hedges and picket fences attempt to provide the level of privacy the houses demand. The whole place reeks of wealth.

We pull into the empty space on the driveway of number four, the house with the red door. A dark blue Volvo estate, complete with roof rack and tinted rear windows—which Liam eyes with envy—takes up the other side of the driveway. The gravel crunches under our feet as we approach the paved path and make our way to the door. I take a deep breath and press the doorbell. I always find the moments before breaking a family apart with life-shattering news the worst part of the job. Despite having darkened many doors with horrendous news and empty platitudes, I find each one just as hard as the last.

A woman answers, and at the sight of two police officers, sinks to the floor, her back against the door. A loud wail escapes her lips as she looks heavenward, tears already pouring down her cheeks.

'Please, no,' she repeats, her voice rising to the edge of hysteria.

Liam grasps her under the shoulder and helps her to her feet, leading her down the wide hallway and into a spacious living room. He walks her over to one of the comfortable seats and eases her into it. She is still crying and seems to be almost on the verge of a panic attack. Liam kneels down beside her, looks her in the eye and, with a soothing voice, attempts to calm her down.

While he is doing this, I leave the living room. Liam is amazing at this part of the job, whereas I am slightly awkward. Also, it never helps the upset person having a bystander gawking at them while they are trying to compose themselves. I make my way to the kitchen, which is at the back of the house.

The airy room is expensively decorated. Black floor tiles and white cupboard doors lend the room a clinical feel, complementing the dark green paint on the walls. A wide American style fridge-freezer fills one wall and other metallic appliances have been built into the furniture. Light streams in through French doors which lead to a colourful, well-kept garden; full of flowers in bloom. A marble topped island fills the middle of the room and houses a coffee machine and an ornate set of mugs.

Ignoring the machine, I boil the kettle and make three cups of tea, before placing them on a tray and making my way back into the living room.

The woman has stopped her howling, and is now sitting quietly, staring with unfocussed eyes at a space on the far side of the room. I place one of the mugs on a little table beside her seat and take my place on the sofa beside Liam.

'Mrs Burston, my name is Detective Inspector Erika Piper. This is Detective Sergeant Liam Sutton. We're sorry to have to tell you that we found the body of your husband, Clive Burston, last night. We are very sorry for your loss.'

The news prompts great, wracking sobs and, once again, Liam gets down on his knees beside her and holds her hands in his. After a few moments, she calms down and takes a number of deep breaths, before wiping away the tears and drawing herself up to her full height.

'How can I help?' she asks, her voice thick with emotion, yet determined.

Over the years, DCI Bob has talked about Clive and Barbara, and I remember him telling me that she was a head teacher in a school in the middle of a rough estate for a long time. Now that she is seemingly in control of her emotional reactions, she has assumed an authoritative air, and for that I am thankful, as it could be helpful for the investigation.

'Can you tell us about Clive's actions over the past month?' I venture.

'You mean, since he made the mistake at work? Well, he's been like a different man, and understandably so. He's never been one to let things get to him, but he's been so down in the dumps. I haven't been able to get him out of his funk.'

'And how did that manifest itself?' asks Liam.

'Well, he spent a lot of time in his office with the door closed. He hadn't left the house in over three weeks. He started to have a few brandies earlier in the day. He was very quiet, uninterested in anything.'

Whilst she continues to discuss his sullen behaviour, I take the time to study the room. A TV sits in the corner, disproportionately small compared to the vastness of the space, showing perhaps that watching TV was far down their list of priorities. An ornate mirror hangs above a fireplace, the mantelpiece covered in picture frames. I rise from the sofa and move closer to take them in. They document a long life lived together as a duo.

Clive peers out at me from different eras—the happiness and contentment radiating off his face. As I set a recent picture of he and his wife blowing out the candles of a sixtieth birthday cake, silence falls in the room.

'Was he well, medically?' I ask, retaking my place beside Liam.

'Yes. He was very healthy for his age. He played squash weekly with a friend from work. He did have an appointment booked to attend the hospital next week, though.'

She rises from her seat and goes to a sideboard. From a very orderly drawer, she produces a letter, which she hands to me. I scan it, taking in the pertinent details.

'He was worried he had dementia?'

'Yes,' she said. 'His mother suffered with it, and after his mishap at work, he was concerned. Of course, he tried to pass it off as simply becoming a tad forgetful with age, but after thirty-seven years of marriage, I could tell something was up.'

'Do you know what he was doing when he was locked in his office?' I ask.

She shakes her head. 'No, he was very secretive. I know he was doing something on his computer, because when I asked to use it, he would go up to the room first before I was allowed on it.'

I consider this information. Perhaps he was trying to keep track of the charges being levelled against him. Perhaps he was having an affair. Though this seems unlikely, considering her assertions that he hadn't left the house in weeks prior to last night. The most likely option was that he was researching the disease he was worried he may be afflicted with, and didn't want to spread his panic to his wife.

'I think the computer will have to be taken for investigation.' I say, and she nods. Her lip trembles slightly.

'Where did you find him?' she asks. The question comes out as a quiver.

'Does the name Marcus Sharpe mean anything to you?' I reply, answering question with question.

Barbara shakes her head.

'He was found in his home. Have you heard of the Bennett Street Rebels?'

Again, she shakes her head.

'They are a gang based in the east side of Manchester. Marcus was a member, so we will be looking at possible links between Clive and the gang.'

'I doubt you'll find anything,' she replies. 'That wasn't his area.'

We descend into silence and I decide that we have probably got everything out of her that we will.

'I think we have taken up enough of your time. You've been very helpful and once again, I am very sorry for your loss.' We get up and Liam leads us towards the front door.

'Did he suffer?' she asks meekly. Her voice sounds like it is on the verge of cracking.

'We don't think so,' I answer truthfully, sparing her the specifics. She thanks me as she shakes my hand, before closing the door behind us. My heart breaks as I imagine her walking down the hallway and into her cavernous living room, contemplating a life without the man she has loved for over four decades.

As we unlock the car, a man comes hurrying across from the house opposite. He is probably in his early fifties, and I assume from the haste with which he has left his garden, he is the street's busybody. For some reason, I imagine a Scooby-Doo villain; hiding behind the fence with eye-holes cut into the wood. The ridiculous thought makes me want to laugh in his face. He extends his hand and introduces himself as Stephen.

'Is Clive dead?' he asks.

'What would give you that impression?' I reply.

'Well, you see, two police officers generally don't turn up on a doorstep with good news.' His voice is high-pitched and nasally.

'How do you know we are police officers?' I ask.

'I saw you hold up your badges. I thought that only happened in the movies,' he laughs.

I decide that I don't like this nosy bastard. I can already imagine him gleefully passing from house to house like some sort of ghoul, delivering the devastating news to the other neighbours.

'He came to see me last night, you see.' My face must show my surprise, as his looks thrilled at catching me cold. 'Yes, I was out mowing my grass in the early evening and he was going out in his car.'

'That car,' I ask, pointing to the Volvo in the driveway.

'No, you see, that's the one Barbara tends to drive. No, he had a red Audi. Often came squealing around the corner into the cul-de-sac. Anyway, I hadn't seen him out of the house in a good while, you see, so I stopped what I was doing and made my way over. He seemed very low, didn't say much, but what he did say was very telling.'

He has me where he wants me. He knows that I am hanging on his every word and he is revelling in it. Though, I swear if he says 'you see' again, I will not be responsible for my actions. Liam can sense my mood and intervenes.

'And what did he say to you, Mr..?'

'Mr Maitland. But please, call me Stephen. Well, I asked him how he'd been and he seemed to well up. He didn't even reply to that.'

'Mr Maitland... Stephen,' Liam corrects himself, as the nosy neighbour is about to intervene with a wagging finger, 'as I'm sure you are aware, we are under a bit of time pressure here, so can you please just tell us what he said to you?'

Stephen looks like the wind has been taken out of his sails. When he speaks, to his credit, he gives the abridged interaction.

'Take care of her,' he replies with a sigh. 'And then he was gone.'

WHISPERS IN THE DARK

6

THE CAR JOURNEY back to the east side of the city, not far from the street where the two bodies were found, is spent in near silence. Liam offered to drive and I readily agreed, pleased to have time to mull over what we have learned so far.

As we swirl around the grey motorway slip road, Clive's final words to his neighbour swim across my vision time and time again—*take care of her*. I consider his mindset, and it makes me wonder if he knew he was setting out to die that night. Did he know, when he was getting into the car, that he would not be coming back? Did he leave his attractive cul-de-sac with murder on his mind? Or suicide? What the hell happened in that room?

A long sigh escapes my lips as my little jigsaw of questions fails to slot together to create even a hint of an answer.

My attention is pulled away from the jarring theories revolving in my head and into the present by the blast of a car horn. A boy racer in a blue souped-up Citroen Saxo wheel-spins out of the junction we are about to enter, almost colliding with the side of our unmarked police car. He extends his middle finger and roars with laughter as he speeds off down the road. I assume, from this welcome, that we have arrived at our destination.

A pair of rectangular concrete blocks, separated by a narrow strip of grass and a vast expanse of a car park, stretch high into the cloudless sky. Hundreds of front doors with small, circular windows peer down onto the stretch of asphalt, populated by an odd mixture of cars. We pull up in a space between a heavily modified Ford Fiesta with a spoiler wider than the car itself and a rusted Renault Clio that would not look out of place in the scrapyard, and exit our own car.

We cross the car park and enter the set of flats on our left. The reception area is uninviting; yellowing linoleum and dirty, once-white painted walls. The stale smell of urine mingled with recently lit marijuana attacks the nostrils. We cross the small room and I press the button to call the lift, wincing as my finger comes away wet. I watch the digital number on the cracked screen above the lift count down slowly to 0, and click my fingers as the lift doors slide open.

'Magic,' I whisper, eliciting a little chuckle from Liam.

As the lift doors close, I can't help but think I'd been quick to condemn the reception area. Compared to the interior of the lift, it could be confused for a fancy Mayfair hotel. The buttons on the console are coated in a sticky film and Liam does the chivalrous thing, stretching his coat over his hand and prodding the button with supersonic speed. The doors creak as they meet in the middle and the lift shudders into action, climbing precariously before coming to an abrupt stop at floor three.

Liam and I exit the lift and step out onto a covered outside balcony; a flimsy looking railing runs the length of the walkway, more an illusion of safety than anything else. Filthy, waterlogged lights, mounted to the ceiling, buzz as we make our way past badly maintained doors towards number 306, the home of Marcus' girlfriend, Kylie Webster.

Loud music blares from behind the door, and as I rap my knuckles on the thin wood, the door belonging to the neighbour at 305 flies open. The head of a man with grey hair and a thick moustache emerges around the door frame, rubbing his eyes.

'Friends of hers, are ya?' he shouts, to which I shake my head. 'Well, whoever you are, tell her to turn the fucking racket down. I'm on night shift.' With that, he slams his door shut, just as Kylie's opens.

'What do you want?' Kylie asks.

I gasp as I turn to take her in. Short denim shorts expose long, fake-tanned legs and a brightly patterned crop top which shows off a toned midriff. Tousled, dyed silver hair falls over her shoulders. A liberal amount of make-up has been applied to her face, in an attempt to cover up the black eye she has sustained recently. The bruising is dark and vivid.

'My name is DI Erika Piper and this is…' I start.

'I don't care about your names, what do you want?' she interrupts, looking up from her phone briefly.

'I have some news about Marcus, may we come in and discuss…'

Again, I am interrupted before I can finish my sentence.

'Look, I don't care what the useless twat has done now. We broke up last night, and I want nothing more to do with him. He's someone else's responsibility now.' She attempts to shut the door, but I manage to get my foot in the way before it can close.

'I didn't want to do this on the doorstep,' I say, 'but Marcus was found dead last night.'

The news doesn't seem to unsettle her too much. She exhales loudly, though more in a 'teenager has just been asked to tidy her room and it's a minor inconvenience' way, than a 'young woman has just found out the boyfriend she very recently broke up with is no longer with us' way.

'You'd best come in then,' she utters. She releases her hold on the door and it swings open slowly on its hinges, exposing a cramped, narrow hallway, made smaller by a number of filled bin bags that have been stacked on top of each other. We cross the threshold and follow her into a poky living room containing mismatched furniture and a ripped leather sofa, which gives the flat a run-down feel. She throws herself onto the sofa, whilst Liam stands awkwardly in the middle of the room. I turn the volume knob on a small stereo system, quietening the pulsating dance music with the chipmunk vocals, and join my partner.

'How'd he die then?' she asks, sounding almost bored.

I cast my gaze over her and can't work out whether she is being petulant on purpose, or if this is just her personality.

'I was hoping you could help us with that. We found some text messages on Marcus' phone that were a little concerning.'

The flash of guilt that passes across her face informs me that she knows exactly what I'm talking about. She sets her phone on the sofa and sits up a little straighter. I can see the beginnings of tears in the corner of her eyes.

'I was angry. We do this shit all the time. We fight, we break up, we make up. But last night he went too far, he hit me. There isn't a way back from that. So, I sent him packing.'

'And then threatened to kill him?' Liam asks.

'I was just pissed off that he wasn't answering my texts.'

She picks up her phone and sets it down almost immediately, as if the device could in some way incriminate her further. I lean down next to her and flash her my most reassuring smile.

'Kylie, can you run us through what happened yesterday?'

'He came here about three. He'd already been drinking and he was high. He brought some gear over here, but I told him that my dad would kill me if he got a whiff of the drugs. He called me boring and we got into a fight and then he hit me,' she says, pulling back her hair so that I can see the full extent of the damage. 'Then he walked out without another word. I sent him a load of texts, making sure he knew that we would never be getting back together. When he didn't reply to any of them, I threatened him. But I didn't mean it. I was just trying to get a reaction.'

I believe her.

'What time did he leave here?' I ask.

'Just before half eight.'

So, we have a time frame for the deaths. From here, it would've taken Marcus about ten minutes to walk to his home, where his murder took place. This means that the violent demise of Marcus and Clive must've taken place between 20:40 and 23:00, when the bodies were discovered by Daniel.

'Is this your house?'

'I rent it, yeah.'

'And do you live alone?'

She nods.

'Were you alone last night, after Marcus left?'

'No,' she replies. 'I called my dad and he came round.'

'Did he stay all night?'

'Yeah, he kipped over. I think I heard him going out at some stage, probably for more beer, judging by the empties in the kitchen this morning.'

Despite her rude welcome, I can now see that Kylie is simply a scared young woman who was being defensive on account of recent happenings. I'm warming to her; I can feel the protective side of my personality taking over.

'Can you think of anyone who would've wanted to hurt Marcus?' Liam asks.

To my surprise, she chuckles. An empty, humourless chuckle.

'Loads of people would love to have hurt him. I imagine the person who has killed him is cracking open a celebratory beer. Marcus told me that he was selling drugs on Olly Pilkington's patch, and was going to keep selling there. I told him it was a stupid idea. Olly has a reputation, you know?'

'Was he dealing drugs for long?'

'No,' she says, shaking her head. 'His mate gave him some and told him that there was demand in that area.'

'Did he tell you about his encounter with Olly Pilkington?'

A look of confusion registers on her face just as the front door opens with a loud click, which prompts Kylie to pull her hair as far across her eye as possible.

'Kylie, love,' booms a deep voice I recognise instantly, 'I think we're going to be OK. It's all been sorted.' The man then begins to whistle a jolly tune as he walks from the hallway into the kitchen. The rustling of plastic suggests he has been to the shops and has returned with bags of food.

'Dad, you best come in here,' shouts Kylie.

The jaunty whistling continues as he makes his way from the kitchen towards his daughter, towards us. The jingle dies in his throat as he enters the room and spots Liam and me—the grin that was plastered across his face falling to a frown.

'Greg. Nice to see you again,' I say, with a smile. 'I think we should have a little chat down at the station, don't you?'

GREG WEBSTER IS a tall, muscular man with a chequered past, though presently he is slouched over the table, his bearded face resting in the palms of his hands. Short, dark hair frames a large forehead marked by scars of bygone disagreements. He looks almost Neanderthal.

He is well known to the police as a former leader of the Longsight Lunatics and for the crime which earned him his notoriety in the first place; the manslaughter of his own father when he was just sixteen years old. He has been in and out of jail his whole life, and has only recently been released from his latest, albeit minor sentence.

I've interviewed Greg personally many times over the years. Usually by now, he would be giving it the big one, making a scene, trying to swing at anyone who comes within arm's length. Today, he seems different. Gone is the arrogance and the intimidation. I begin the recording.

'Where were you last night, Greg?'

'I was at my daughter's house. Comforting her.' He points to his eye, the same eye that Kylie had blackened by her boyfriend last night.

'All night?'

'Mmmhmm,' he nods.

'You see, Kylie mentioned that she heard you leave at some point. Does that ring a bell?'

He nods again. 'I nipped to the corner shop for cigarettes and some booze. Was only gone for ten minutes. When I came back, I went up to check on her and she must've cried herself to sleep. It was the first time all night that she finally looked at peace.'

A sudden flash of sickness rises in my stomach. I put my hand to my mouth and wait for the feeling to pass, though the feeling only intensifies. Greg looks perplexed as I push myself out of the chair and rush from the room, leaving Liam and him alone.

As I make my way to the toilet, I see Angela, another Detective Sergeant, leave the control room and make her way to the interview room, to take my place.

I make it to the bathroom, but not the toilet, as the contents of my stomach empty over the floor.

7

THE QUEASINESS WHICH forced me home last night and prevented me from finishing the interview with Greg Webster has not abated. In fact, as the early morning light swims into the room through the thin linen curtains, I can feel the sickness swirling in my stomach with even more fervour. I leap out of bed and just manage to kneel beside the toilet before vomiting into the bowl.

Once I'm sure that I am finished, I push myself to my feet and make my way to the sink. I squeeze a liberal amount of toothpaste onto the brush and plunge it into my mouth. I consider what I have eaten over the past 24 hours and can't think of anything that would cause such a violent bout of sickness. Tom, who has consumed the same meals as I have, is fine. I set the toothbrush back on the shelf and return to bed, pulling the covers over me and cosying into Tom's bare chest.

'You OK?' he mumbles, his voice deep with sleep.

I nod my head and curl my fingers through the coarse hair that runs from his stomach to his chest.

'What do you think is causing it?'

Since the sickly feeling had stretched long into the night, leaving me unable to sleep, I had spent a lot of time on my phone, using the time with Doctor Google to self-diagnose. Because of a heightened sense of smell and a feeling akin to motion sickness, I'd discounted food poisoning or gastritis. Many articles appeared suggesting morning sickness, which caused me to break out in a cold sweat.

Whilst recuperating from an almost fatal stabbing nearly two years ago, the doctors had dealt me the crushing news that I was highly unlikely to ever be a mother. They had put my chances of conceiving at around five percent, and I had felt that figure was just one they chose to cover the fact they were doing all they could to not use the word 'impossible'. However, having read the symptoms of morning sickness, I couldn't help but think that this was sounding closest to the mark.

'I don't know,' I reply, noncommittally. For some ridiculous reason, voicing my theory seems like a form of self-betrayal.

'Are you in work today?' he asks, half-changing the subject.

'Liam and I are going to see Olly Pilkington,' I answer, sighing and pulling myself out of bed again as my phone pings on the other side of the room. I pull the charging cable out of the port and sit down on the end of the bed.

'Speak of the devil,' I say as I pull my dressing gown over my pyjamas. 'Liam has just sent through the recording of the interview with Greg. I'm going to go down to the kitchen and have a listen.'

Tom mumbles a sleepy reply and rolls over, already dead to the world as his head makes contact with the pillow again.

I tiptoe out of the room and head down the stairs towards the kitchen. Tom and I have been living together for around three months, though we have been dating for just over eight. With his rental agreement nearing its end, and my housing situation up in the air following the end of my previous relationship, we felt the forces of nature pushing us together, so he moved in with me.

Neither of us are commitment-phobes and we reasoned that if it didn't work out between the two of us, he could simply move out again. Though, there is no reason to think that there is going to be a problem. Currently, and it could be the honeymoon period of the relationship talking, it's the best relationship I've ever been in. It's like Tom has been designed especially for me.

I make a strong cup of coffee and sit down at the kitchen table, opening my laptop and logging into my email account. I open the file that Liam had recently sent through and it begins to download. I take a sip from my coffee and think about Greg Webster.

A new window opens automatically on my computer screen and the video begins to play of its own accord. I settle back into my seat, ready to watch the unfolding theatre. I fast forward to the part where I clasp my hand to my face and abandon ship. As I escape out of the door, Liam and Greg exchange a confused look, and DS Angela Poynter enters, quickly occupying the empty seat. Liam, ever the professional, is only momentarily distracted from the line of questioning.

Greg claims that, after returning from the corner shop, he had checked Kylie was asleep and then spent the rest of the evening in the living room, making sure she was safe and that Marcus didn't return. He called it a night at around midnight and slept on the sofa. During the rest of the interview, he also asserts that he was referring to paying an electricity bill when he had entered the house and told Kylie they were in the clear and that what he said was entirely unrelated to Marcus' demise. The biggest revelation is saved for the final few minutes of the video. Apparently, during his most recent stretch of jail time, Greg had become disillusioned with life. He knew he had to make a change. So, he went to the prison's church.

At first he was just curious, but each week, he went back and by the end, he had been baptised and become a Christian. He tells Liam that he knows he has not been a good man in the past and is very sorry for the grief he has caused the police over the years, but now he is a changed man. He has sworn off the gangs and he knows that keeping out of trouble 'on the outside', as he puts it, will be difficult, but that he really wants to make a good go of it. I can tell by Liam's furrowed brow, captured on the recording, that he is struggling to believe this admission.

'READY?' LIAM ASKS, as we pull up outside the home of Olly Pilkington, leader of the Longsight Lunatics.

A bright orange car with black racing stripes, presumably belonging to the man we are here to see, on account of the personalised number plate 011 P1LK, is parked in the driveway of the end-of-terrace house. An imposing wooden fence wraps its way around the perimeter of the property, though a narrow gate grants us access to an overgrown patio area, which the weeds are attempting to claim as their own. A number of wooden doors from an old wardrobe, one with a mirror attached, lie discarded on the paving stones. A rusted Sky dish hangs uncertainly above our heads from a single frayed wire and a sign warning us of the presence of dogs has been drilled into the wall beside the front door. Liam knocks.

The sound of chains rattling and scraping against their holds signifies that someone is about to open the door. Eventually, the well-protected door swings open and a man in his early thirties with shaved ginger hair and a diamond earring stands in the opening, his heavily tattooed arms folded across his muscular chest. He squints into the early afternoon sun, raising a hand to his forehead, trying to work out who we are. I decide to spare him the effort.

'Mr Pilkington, my name is DI Erika Piper and this is DS Liam Sutton. May we come in?'

'Get to fuck,' he spits with venom, attempting to close the door. Liam takes a quick step forward and shoves his shoulder into the door, knocking Olly off balance.

'We only want to have a chat,' Liam says.

'We've got no need to chat, I've not done owt,' Olly replies, steadying himself on the banister of the stairs and pulling himself up to his full height, which comes to near Liam's nose.

'We haven't said you've done anything. We just want a few minutes of your time and we thought you'd prefer to do that here, in the comfort of your home, rather than at the station. But...'

'Oh, for fuck's sake, come in then,' Olly interrupts.

He walks away from the door and we follow him into a messy living room dominated by a huge television currently showing animated soldiers battling to keep hold of territory. Olly picks up a gaming controller and pauses it, the fighters frozen in time. He sits down on a tatty beanbag on the floor and picks up a cigarette which had been resting in an ashtray. Discarded clothes, empty crisp bags and bottles of beer litter the floor. Liam and I take a seat on the uncomfortable sofa.

'How can I help you then officers?' he asks.

'Does the name Marcus Sharpe mean anything to you?' says Liam.

Olly takes a few moments to think, or at least make it look like he's thinking, before shaking his head. I unfold a picture of him and show him it. Again, he shakes his head.

'We know you paid him a visit a few weeks ago.'

Olly looks confused.

'Paid this guy a visit?' he replies, pointing to the picture that I'm still holding up. 'I don't think so, I ain't ever seen him before.'

'We have it on record that you visited his house a few weeks ago, threatened him and then used a knife as a weapon on him. What do you say to that?'

He stubs the cigarette out in the ashtray on the floor and immediately takes another from a packet lying close to him. He lights it and blows a plume of smoke in our direction.

'I'd say prove it.' He taps the cigarette on the edge of the ashtray, though some of the ash drifts onto the floor. He then fixes us with a stare in turn, first Liam, then me. 'I'll say it once more, because apparently this doesn't seem to be filtering into your thick fucking skulls; I have never seen this guy before.'

'The interesting thing is,' I continue, trying not to rise to his incredible level of rudeness, though I of course would love to knock that shit-eating grin off his face with the nearest heavy object, 'is that he was found murdered. A few weeks after your purported visit, warning him off your patch.'

He gets up from his beanbag and stands to face us. Liam stands too, though Olly doesn't seem to be intimidated. I remain sitting, just to bring some balance to the exchange.

'Get to the point,' he says.

'Where were you on Saturday, the third of August, between eight and eleven?'

'Right here,' he says.

'Could anyone verify this?'

'They could,' he replies, 'but they don't need to 'cos I'm telling you and I'm not a liar.'

Liam takes a step forward.

'You're doing yourself no favours with the attitude,' he says. Even though Liam and Olly are around the same age, it is like watching an exchange between a weary father and a temperamental son. Though, of course, I think Liam might take offence at that particular analogy.

Olly closes the gap further between the two and swings his head towards Liam, stopping just before contact is made.

'And you're doing yourself no favours barging into my gaff and accusing me of something you ain't got no proof of, you fucking queer,' he barks. 'I don't know who that fella is, I haven't seen him before and whoever lied to you, telling you I was in his house, is in for a world of trouble if I ever find out who it was.'

Liam holds firm and both men lock eyes like they are about to weigh in at a boxing match. Eventually, Liam takes a step back, thanks him for his time, and we leave.

'How does he know I'm gay?' Liam asks, as we get back into the car. I simply shrug my shoulders, unwilling to point out that not many policemen wear a matching shirt and pocket square to work.

AFTER THE VISIT to Olly's house, the rest of the day had been spent on paperwork. I'd requested the CCTV camera footage from both entrances to Marcus' street and done some more digging into Clive's mistakes, which didn't seem to be anything to do with events happening in Manchester. I'd also called his wife to ask if he was left-handed, as I'd forgotten to pose that question when we had visited her. She'd confirmed that he was and wondered what that had to do with the case, to which I couldn't give an adequate answer.

Presently, I find Tom's number in my phone. Having quit the police force after being abducted and almost killed by the crazed author last year, Tom was now working as a security guard. Currently, he was on shifts at a film set location in the Northern Quarter area of Manchester, though I knew we were both going to be in tonight—something that I was looking forward to. After a quick phone call, in which we decide on frozen pizza and some garlic bread for tea, I make my way around the supermarket collecting items and tossing them into the basket.

I find that I have wandered to the cosmetics aisle and I don't know if I've brought myself here consciously or subconsciously, but I am face to face with pregnancy tests. The sickness had gone away as the day had worn on, but I couldn't shake the feeling of hope. The articles I read last night; the ones accompanied with pictures of tiny feet and impossibly small hands wrapped around an adult finger swim into my vision.

With shaking hands, I pick one up and put it into the basket carefully before shaking my head and setting it back on the shelf. I feel like I am playing with my emotions, emotions I worked hard at sealing in a box and filing away. Now, here I am, threatening to unpick all that hard work.

Though, there is cause to wonder. The recent sickness coupled with my late period—which I'd simply attributed to a symptom of my operation two years ago—now make me question if there is something else in it. I take a deep breath before picking the pregnancy test up again and walking to the till before I can change my mind.

8

ONE LINE.

One thin blue line to show that the test has worked.

One space where another thin blue line could go.

One line means it's negative.

One line means my ridiculous notion that I could somehow mother a child is exactly that—ridiculous. I'd allowed a bout of sickness, most probably a twenty-four-hour bug, to fool me into thinking that I knew better than the doctors; medical professionals who put my chances at having a baby at 'needing a miracle' level.

Tom had held me as I'd sobbed long into the night, mourning a child that had only ever been a figment of my imagination. I'd listened as he told me about the same thing happening to his sister, how there wasn't enough, something—he couldn't remember the word, in her urine for it to show up on the test. He begged me to stay positive and to try again in a week's time, but I shook my head. My little folly of trying to convince myself that my body was capable of something ground-breaking was over. I'd remained awake as his breathing became deeper and his grip on my side became loose, though I must've finally drifted into a light sleep as the alarm ringing on the other side of the room forces me out of bed and into the shower.

As the water washes away the memory of yesterday, I resolve myself to focus fully on the case. We have two bodies, no leads and that needs to change.

The poor ventilation in the meeting room is particularly obvious on a fine Summer's day. Sunlight streams in through the glass and, even though it has barely passed ten o'clock, most of the assembled team have removed their jackets and rolled up their sleeves. The smell of sweat is prominent.

I promise everyone that I will be as fast as I can and wheel the case board into the centre of the room for everyone to see. Pictures of various men stare out at the gathered officers.

I start with a picture of the crime scene; one body slumped on top of the other. Most have seen it already, but sometimes revisiting the case from the start can bear fruit. Pictures of Marcus and Clive, alive and well, are pinned above it. Angela stands up and tells the room that after exhausting police records, she hasn't been able to find a link between the two men. Aside from featuring in an anti-social behaviour report four years ago, Marcus seems to have done well at keeping out of trouble. Even then, he was part of a group and not one of the main names mentioned by the resident of Bennett Street. Angela surmises that even if Marcus were a main player in the gang, Clive would never have been involved in their arrests, owing to the fact that he was in charge of a completely different area.

We move on to the other two photographs on the board, starting with the man with the short ginger hair and armfuls of tribal tattoos—Olly Pilkington. Most officers in the room let out a sigh or an expletive when I point to him, the gang boss who has caused each one hassle at some stage in their careers and needs no introduction. I inform the team about his motive, how Marcus was selling on his patch, and about Olly's alleged visit to Marcus' house. Angela makes a note to try and find out from Daniel if he can remember the date of Olly's appearance in the house, possibly in the hope of CCTV catching him in the area. However much Olly and Marcus didn't see eye to eye, it seems the leader of the Longsight Lunatics had no reason to murder DCI Clive Burston.

Which leaves Greg Webster, who may have motive to murder both. As a father, I can only imagine the rage he must've felt upon seeing his daughter's black eye, doled out by a deadbeat, drug dealer boyfriend from a rival gang. I explain that, apparently, he has left that life behind after finding salvation, but I wonder aloud if perhaps this incident had tipped him over the edge.

We know he left the house during the time window of the murders; he has admitted to that, though he said it was only briefly and he only visited the corner shop. He is also the only man in our field of vision at the minute who has a connection to Clive, having traded blows with him when Clive was a DI in the city and when Greg was just setting up the gang which would go on to be the Longsight Lunatics.

I finish the briefing, no clearer as to the next step in the investigation, but happy in the knowledge that there are a few strands to follow and that capable officers are the ones pursuing them. I leave the sweatbox and walk across the open plan area to my office, closing the door behind me. I sit down on my chair and power up the computer.

Whilst it installs urgent updates against my will, I reach into my bag and pull out the foil strip of tablets. The pace of the investigation so far; the early mornings and late nights, had lessened my dependence on the tablets and I'm coping with taking the required amount, but hitting this dead end coupled with the disappointment of the failed pregnancy test was hard to take. I push one of the tablets out and notice that it is my last. Fuck. I consider saving it for tomorrow in case I can't get an emergency prescription later on, but the lure of the little sugar-coated capsule is too much. I gulp it down and stifle a cough just as there is a knock on my door and Liam pokes his head around the frame. He looks at me quizzically.

'Everything OK, partner?'

I nod.

'The CCTV for Bennett Street has just arrived from Friday night. Do you want me to look through it or do you want to?' he asks.

'I'd like to have a look. Can you send it over?'

He nods before closing the door. I realise that I must look sweaty from being in the briefing room, and my cheeks are probably red from coughing. I'm also not great at hiding a look of guilt. I pick the empty foil packet up and put it back in my bag.

A minute later, two files land in my inbox and I double click on one, which opens into a screen sized window. The black-and-white video shows a panoramic view of the junction I had used to enter Bennett Street on the night the bodies were discovered. The long street is opposite the camera's position and is flanked by the gothic church on the left and a row of shops and takeaways on the right. The timestamp shows that the footage begins at seven o'clock. I set the speed to double time.

Traffic zooms by at twice the speed limit, and people enter and leave the shops to the right. A father and son go into a fast-food restaurant, order and take a seat in the window. They laugh and joke and continue to do so once their meal arrives. At just after half-past eight, Marcus walks unsteadily into view. He sits on the wall of the church and fishes a cigarette out of his pocket, before lighting it. A group of lads walk by and some of them give Marcus an elaborate handshake. They exchange some friendly-looking words, on account of the nodding and laughing, before moving out of view.

Marcus then pushes himself off the wall, turns around and peers into the grounds of the church before making his way up the street towards his house. Unfortunately, his house is too far up the street to be able to follow his journey further.

During the remainder of the video, too many cars and people turn in and out of the street to be able to take note of. However, neither Greg nor Olly appear to be present. Unless, of course, they used a car not known to the police to get close to the house. The only way of knowing is to check every car's number plate to make sure they are not associated with our two suspects. It's a time-consuming job, but at the minute it's the only lead we've got. I exit

WHISPERS IN THE DARK

out of the video and send an email to one of the members of the team to get started on this course of action.

I then open the other file. It is a video from the far end of the street. It's from a similar vantage point, except the houses at either end are flanked by trees, rather than shops and places of worship. Again, Marcus' house is too far down the row of terraces to be able to see, and there are too many cars to take note of that access the street from this direction. However, two things of interest are to be found from this camera.

One: At quarter past eight, a car matching the description that that nosy neighbour gave us of Clive's metallic red Audi Q7 indicates and pauses in the road, waiting for a gap in the passing traffic. The number plate also matches that of the one registered on the police's database. The car then enters the street and drives out of the camera's view.

Two: At ten past nine, a man walks past the camera with a beanie hat pulled low over his forehead. Because of this and the direction of travel, it's hard to make out any distinguishing features. He walks down the street at pace and out of view. Ten minutes later, the same man hurries back up the street towards the camera and it's then, while he's twirling his hat in his hands, that I get a good look at him.

It's none other than Greg Webster.

9

'I DIDN'T THINK it was relevant.'

'You didn't think it was relevant?' I repeat incredulously.

Greg's lip juts out and he throws his hands in the air. His open shirt collar is pulled wide, revealing a thin gold necklace with a cross pendant hanging from it that wasn't there yesterday. I assume this is meant to show his devotion to God. Cynically though, I wonder if this is some form of subliminal messaging he has employed to make me believe he is fully dedicated to the Almighty, leaving his life of crime behind him. Taking into account how willingly he came to the station for a second interview, I'm almost inclined to give him the benefit of the doubt.

'Greg. Listen to me. This is serious. Two men you have a connection to are dead...'

'I know,' he interrupts. 'That's why I'm here, to show you that I have nothing to do with this and to clear my name.'

'So do that. Here's what I know so far. DCI Clive Burston drove into Bennett Street, presumably to visit Marcus Stone. There is no apparent connection between the two men, so the meaning of their meeting is an absolute mystery to us at the minute. Thirty-five minutes later, you enter the same street. Ten minutes after that, you leave and a little while later, both are found dead. You failed to disclose this information last time...'

'Because I just told you I didn't think it was relevant,' he says, slightly louder than before. He always was a hot-head and I can see that he is trying to keep a lid on it, but some colour has sprung into his cheeks and his brow has creased. It seems old habits die hard.

'So, fill me in on those missing ten minutes.'

He exhales loudly and unbuttons the cuffs of his shirt sleeves, making a show of rolling them up to his elbows. He scratches a small area of eczema on his forearm, causing small flecks of skin to fall onto the table. He wipes them onto the floor with the back of his hand.

'After I'd seen Kylie's eye, I'll admit, I wanted to kill Marcus. When she went to her room, I decided I'd nip to the shop for some cigarettes, and I did. But my feet had a mind of their own. I found myself at the end of his road and thought I'd pay him a visit, just to tell him that this time it was definitely over. No going back.'

'So, you did speak to him?' Liam asks.

Greg looks annoyed at having his story interrupted.

'No, I'm getting to that,' he answers, fixing Liam with a glare. 'I knocked on his door, but there was no answer. I looked in the living room window and I knew he was in, because the lights were on. I knocked a few more times, but still no answer so I cut my loses and left.'

'Did you hear anything from inside?'

He shakes his head.

'So, you just left? Didn't decide to kick the door in, or leave a little note or anything the old Gregory Webster would've been inclined to do?' I ask.

He laughs. 'The old Gregory Webster would've poured petrol through the letterbox and burnt the little fucker alive. The new Gregory Webster has a much more level head on his shoulders, thanks to the grace of God. No, like I say, all I wanted was a quiet word with him. I knocked, and I left.'

'What are you doing for work, now that you're out?' Liam asks.

Greg looks surprised, caught off guard by the personal nature of the question.

'I'm working in IT. When I was inside, they found out our interests and set up a sort of apprenticeship. I was always handy with computers, so I was keen to get involved with Byte It...'

'Byte It?'

'That's the name of the company. It's based in the city centre, near Clarence Street, just by the town hall. My job is to try and fix customer's computers remotely, but occasionally I do have to visit.'

I write the name of the company into my notebook and make a note beside it to contact the manager or the owner. Primarily, to make sure that he is telling us the truth. It will also be interesting to hear their view on his past and what his behaviour is like during working hours.

'Do you like it?'

'I do,' he nods. 'I like that I'm doing something legitimate and that I'm helping people. I feel like I've turned over a new leaf. I'm just so thankful that a company like that was willing to take a chance on me. Over the years, I've been met with a lot of derision when attempting to sort a proper job. That's why I kept going back to what I knew.'

After a few more questions about his new job, we thank him for his time and he leaves the room, making his way to the reception area. Though he seems like he is trying hard to lead a fulfilling and crime free life, in my head, the jury is still out.

La Chiesa del Signore is quite busy for a weekday. The popular Italian restaurant is situated in the heart of Marple village and has recently undergone a facelift, the frosted glass and heated outside seating bringing it into the twenty-first century. I wonder if some of that money would have been better spent on hiring more staff, as Tom has been at the bar for so long that I have already perused the menu countless times and chosen all three of my courses. Finally, he returns to the table with a pint of Guinness and a glass of white wine, which he sets in front of me, sloshing a little over the rim.

'Sorry about that,' he says, 'I don't think she's ever poured a pint of the black stuff before. I had to tell her what to do with the head.'

I take a sip from my glass at the same time as Tom. When he pulls his away, thick white foam stays behind, clinging to the stubble above his top lip. He licks it away with a wet tongue and stretches his arms out, content. He removes his hoodie, hangs it on the back of his chair and pushes away some rogue hair that has fallen onto his forehead.

'How's the case going then?' he asks.

I explain the progress, or lack thereof, we have made so far. How aggressive and homophobic Olly Pilkington had been when we had visited him and how Greg Webster has appeared to have turned over a new leaf, though I can't make my mind up whether it is all an act.

A waiter with a crisp white shirt and an authentic Italian accent that rolls off the tongue approaches our table and takes our order, before taking our menus and leaving with a small bow.

'And how are you coping with it all?'

There's a knowing look on his face and I wonder what he is getting at. I assure him that I am coping fine and aside from the frustrations of the case, I'm enjoying the job. When I finish, he looks uneasy.

'There was a message left on the answering machine at home today… from the doctors,' he says.

I can feel my stomach drop and an irrational annoyance with him for checking our answering machine enters my brain and leaves just as quickly.

'I can explain,' I start.

'I don't need you to explain,' he cuts me off. 'I need you to make sure that you are taking the dosage the doctors have told you to. What we went through, in that mill, I get it, okay?'

He reaches across the table and takes my hand in his. My eyes fill with tears at the mention of the mill—the site of two near-death experiences for me. Nearly three years ago, I was stabbed there and left for dead by a masked thug, resulting in a life-saving operation and almost a year off work. Then, eight months ago, I was nearly a footnote of Ed Bennett's murderous quest for a lasting legacy. A sob escapes me just as the waiter returns to our table carrying our starters. I realise that with Tom attempting to console me, it must look like he is breaking up with me. The waiter dumps the plates of garlic bread with less care than I imagine he normally would and vacates our area at speed.

'I'm sorry,' I splutter. 'I'll get it under control.'

He hands me a napkin with which I dab under my eyes and blow my nose.

'I know you will,' he replies. 'Especially now that there might be a baby in there.'

It takes a moment to register what he has said, and when he does, it feels like I've been slapped. 'We know there isn't,' I snap, pushing myself out of my seat and making my way to the stairs which lead to the toilets. I go into one of the cubicles and slide the lock across. The toilet seat feels cold against my bare legs, and I fight to suppress a scream that is waiting to be let out. I use the calming breathing techniques I'd been taught at my therapy session last year and, after a few minutes, I leave the cubicle and look at myself in the mirror. I splash some water on my face and pull my hair into a tight ponytail, before leaving the toilet and ascending the stairs.

Tom's back is to me and when I squeeze his shoulder, he jumps, before grovelling apologies, which I wave away with my hand.

'Look,' I say, sitting back down opposite him, 'my emotions are all over the place at the minute, and I got myself excited about something that I know is almost definitely never going to happen.'

He attempts to interrupt, but I hold my hand up.

'We need to be realistic now. If babies are something you want in your future...'

'I want you,' he interjects, reaching out for my hand again. I feel my eyes well with tears and I get up from my seat to give him a hug. When I retake my seat, we chomp through the garlic bread, though my appetite has diminished somewhat since we ordered. After a while, the waiter, perhaps sensing that it is safe to approach again, comes to the table and removes our cold, half-eaten starters with an uncertain smile.

After the heaviness of the evening so far, we fall into relaxed conversation. He tells me about some of the semi-famous faces he has recognised on the film set he is currently a security guard on and I recount to him some of Sophie's, my sister's baby, latest milestones which include sitting up and rolling over. My appetite returns with a bang as my steaming carbonara and his freshly baked pizza arrives. The conversation stops as we both stuff our faces.

As I'm pouring a glass of water from the jug, my phone rings. I fish it from the front pocket of my bag and despair at the name that is flashing on the screen.

'Hi John, I'm guessing this isn't a social call,' I say.

'No,' he replies, almost apologetically. 'I'm afraid with Bob still side-lined from the case, you're my point of contact.'

'I assume we have another body?' I state.

'We have two.'

10

FROM MY VANTAGE point, the vivid pink and blue striped, cloudless sky is a beautiful backdrop for the Gothic church. However, the roar of traffic from the main road behind me and the abuse from youths passing by on bikes detract from the scene somewhat. Blue and white tape has already been pulled across the various entrances to the church grounds and a number of police cars line the street running parallel to the church—the street where Marcus and Clive's bodies were found only a few days ago. I raise the tape on the main gate and duck under it, entering the grounds of St. Peter & The Light Anglican Church.

A wooden notice board with a Perspex covering protects printed announcements and advertisements; a plea for more members for the church choir; particularly soprano voices, youth fellowship dates, and a schedule of sermons for the upcoming month. Rows of gravestones block the setting sun's light, casting shadows over the roughly paved path which bisects the freshly mowed grass. As I walk over the uneven surface towards the building, I can't help but think that the terrain must pose a challenge for the more elderly members of the congregation.

Heavy wooden doors are held open by rusted hooks, drilled into the wall on either side. A uniformed officer is keeping vigil just outside. Despite the late evening sun, the small entranceway is untouched by any of the remaining heat. It is deathly cold. The room has recently been touched up with a light magnolia, the faint smell of paint lingering in the air. Two flimsy looking doors, both slightly ajar, lead to toilets, an outline of a man and a woman painted at eye-level on each. A number of orders of service from a recent wedding are spread across a vestibule table, and a collection box for a local charity is attached to the table's leg with a thick chain. It's that kind of area.

As I reach for the door handle to gain access to the actual church, Liam strides through the exterior door towards me and recoils at the lack of heat in the room. I give a small wave before handing him one of the protective suits and pulling on my own. When we are fully covered and of no risk of contaminating the crime scene, I yank the door open and gasp at what greets us inside.

The main room of the church is such a juxtaposition to the room we have just been in. Whereas the entranceway lacked any distinguishing features, this room is full of them. The dying embers of the day drift through beautifully patterned stained-glass windows depicting scenes from the Bible. Despite its size, exposed roof-beams lend the room a homely, farmhouse feel. The ends of the heavy wooden pews are ornately carved and an ornamental marble cross with a serene looking Jesus attached to it overlooks the pulpit at the front of the grand space. Next to the pulpit is an organ, its decorative brass pipes of various lengths rising towards the ceiling like pillars of smoke.

I can imagine how all of these elements could combine to create a very Godly air, however, right now, the bodies are bringing the religious atmosphere down a touch.

Two of them.

The first is located at the foot of the pulpit, at the front of the church from where the vicar would address the congregation. He is face down on the thick navy carpet; his head is turned towards me, his left arm stretched straight ahead of him, his right to the side, ushering me closer. His eyes remain open, staring yet unstaring and his mouth forms a little O shape, like he died blowing bubbles. His bright ginger hair and beard are visible from the end of the aisle and, as I walk towards him, I notice something unusual. He isn't wearing any clothes. His nakedness showcases an array of coloured tattoos over his ribs and legs, though the one I was expecting is not present. Or simply not visible yet.

As Liam and I stand over him, it's easy to see the cause of his death. Vicious tears cover his back, still spilling blood onto the carpet. I bend down to get a closer look. Each wound is deep and ragged; some overlap, creating criss-cross effects, making it hard to count the exact number of cuts. The frenzy of the attacker is evident, this poor guy's back has been ripped to shreds.

'How many do you reckon?' asks Liam.

'Hard to tell,' I reply, 'maybe fifteen or sixteen?'

He nods his agreement.

'I counted fourteen,' says a voice to our right, in the corner of the room. John Kirrane steps out of the shadows. 'Though, of course, I could be wrong.'

Very unlikely, I think to myself.

He points to the man's wrists. 'Similar to the burns and markings found on Marcus. In fact, on first look, I'd say the pattern of the binding is identical. He's been photographed and everything has been documented on this side. I wanted you to see the damage before we turned him. Do you need to see any more or shall we flip him over?'

I take one last walk around the body, but with no other apparent injuries, we carefully turn him over. Just as he becomes perpendicular with the floor, the wounds seem to stretch and open up, causing blood to cascade onto the carpet. We quickly lay him on the floor, where he comes to rest with a horrible squelching noise.

The front of the body is covered in blood, but only because he has been lying in a pool of it. It shows no signs of violence. He has a great physique; a defined six-pack and chiselled pecs showing a devotion to the gym. Newly grown, reddish stubble covers his chest, suggesting he has recently shaved it. Perhaps he was a body builder, perhaps just a bit vain. His flaccid penis rests against a chunky thigh and two of the toes on his right foot are crooked; probably broken and reset sometime in the past. On the inside of his bulging left bicep is the Bennett Street Rebels tattoo I'd been looking for.

A pink card, a driving licence, is stuck to his stomach, covering his belly button. With a gloved hand, I pick it up and turn it over, wiping the blood off it, to reveal a clean shaven, unsmiling picture of our victim, taken a few years ago. His intense eyes bore into me. The details reveal that his name is Kai McCormick and on his last birthday, just over a month ago, he turned twenty-two years old. I tap my finger on the picture of his face.

'I recognise him,' I say. 'He was outside Marcus's house, the night I went to the crime scene. He told me I had a nice arse.' Liam laughs and it reverberates around the room, causing a few of the Scene-of-crime officers to look over.

I pass the card to Liam and he spends a minute studying it, before bagging it and calling Martin over, who accepts it and walks back towards his team on the other side of the room.

'So, we're thinking this is the work of the same killer?' Liam asks, pointing at the tattoo.

'Well…' John starts, before trailing off and beckoning us over to where he was before we interrupted him. We follow him, and a trail of blood, to the edge of the room. Down two stone steps, in a darkened archway, is a green door with a brass handle.

A diminutive woman in a formally beige cashmere turtleneck is blocking the way. Her top is so soaked with blood that it appears to have turned black. Exposed wrists show scars of old. Rips in her leather trousers reveal pale skin and double-knotted cream Converse, now stained red, cover her small feet.

A deep wound on the left side of her neck gapes at me.

John points to a bottle green jacket that has been thrown over the front pew. I peel off the bloody gloves and pull my hands into a new, clean pair. I pick the jacket up and carefully feel each of the pockets. When I find what I think I'm looking for, I reach into an inside breast pocket and from it I fish a mobile phone. The lock screen shows a picture of the woman in front of me, having her cheek kissed by a pretty Asian girl. From another pocket, I pull out a purse, inside which I find a bank card which identifies the victim as a Miss Zoe Sullivan.

'I've not had a chance to look this body over,' says John. 'Could you give me ten minutes?'

'Of course,' I reply. 'Do you know who called it in?'

'The vicar, he's through that door.' He points to the far side of the hall, away from the death.

We leave John to cast his expert eye over Zoe's body and walk across the church, dodging various scene-of-crime officers and photographers who are studiously going about documenting the room. Once we get to an identical archway and green door, I knock a few times and let myself and Liam into a small office.

A uniformed officer with bushy, grey sideburns sits awkwardly next to a sobbing man, who must be the vicar. He is wearing civilian clothing and sits on a leather swivel chair. Dark hair, flecked with white, falls onto his forehead. His elbows are resting on a sturdy wooden table that also holds a desktop computer which whirrs quietly, and a monitor which is currently turned off. Many mugs, some with long gone cold tea in them, clutter the desk, suggesting that the vicar spends a lot of time here. His head is in his hands. A clock on the wall opposite us announces each passing second with a loud tick.

Liam and I pull up two chairs and sit facing him. The man lifts his head to look at us with bleary, red eyes. We introduce ourselves and he gives us a little smile.

'It is at times like this, detectives, that I wish I drank,' he says, his voice thick with emotion. He reaches across and shakes our hands with a firm grip that hurts my fingers. 'My name is Richard Clark. I am the vicar here.'

'And you found the bodies?' Liam asks.

He nods and swallows, his Adam's apple rising and falling, the movement accentuated by how clean shaven he is. There is not a hint of a five o'clock shadow.

'Can you tell us how that came about?'

He takes a moment to compose himself. 'I was at home, trying to write my sermon for next week, but I realised that I'd left some notes here. I came here to fetch them and… and…'

'Take your time,' I say, and he nods at me.

'In the darkness, I nearly tripped coming through the door. I thought perhaps someone hadn't cleared away some of the equipment from last night's film event. You see, during the school holidays we run various activities for families in the area. Sorry,' he pauses, 'I'm babbling. Anyway, as I was about to bend down to pick whatever it was up, I realised it was a body. It was like something from a nightmare, here in God's house, of all places. I've never seen anything like it…'

He trails off and his eyes become wet again.

There's a knock on the door and John pokes his head around the door. 'Ready when you are,' he says. I nod my head almost imperceptibly towards the emotional vicar, and John bites his bottom lip as he backs out of the room.

'Mr Clark,' I start, 'when you are ready, I'm going to get someone to come and take a statement from you. I'd appreciate it if we could arrange a time to meet tomorrow. I've got more questions.'

He gives me a weak smile and confirms that he will keep tomorrow free. He gives a feeble wave goodbye.

John is standing over Zoe's body, deep in conversation with a nodding crime scene photographer, whose camera is hanging around his neck. As we approach, the photographer walks away and John motions to the body.

'Ok, so obvious cause of death,' I say, pointing to the neck and John nods his head in agreement.

'What are we thinking here then?' Liam asks. 'Do you reckon these two met up for some kind of sexual liaison?'

'We thought that with the two men at the first crime scene and that turned out to be incorrect. With these two, it's certainly possible,' he replies, 'though unlikely. Forensics will obviously test the fluids on the bodies and semen will be one of the things they will look for.'

'Murder weapon?' I ask.

John shakes his head. 'No sign so far. It bears a lot of similarities to the first crime scene. Two bodies, similar deaths, no murder weapon.'

'So, we're thinking that the killer found them here, perhaps even arranged for them to be here, killed them both and did a runner?' says Liam.

John shakes his head.

'I think the killer is right here,' he says, pointing at Zoe's body. Liam and I both look at him, the doubt written all over our faces. A smile creeps over John's.

He invites us to crouch next to the body, in order to present his theory. Firstly, he focuses on her neck but looks past the gaping hole, instead pointing to several little scrapes that surround it.

'These are what we call *courage marks*. I've seen them countless times on suicide victims. They are the marks left behind as the victim summons up the nerve, the build up to the big finish.'

He then directs our attention to her right hand. It is stained red with blood, blood I assumed was her own.

'Her hand has two gashes on it. These injuries are textbook of a murderer who used a knife. As they stab the victim, the blood makes the knife slippery, and often the killer cuts their own hand. When we test the male's body, I'd be very surprised if her blood is not also present.'

'So, let me get this straight,' says Liam. 'You're saying that you think Zoe killed Kai?'

John nods.

'And if that's your theory on this scene, I'm guessing you also think that Clive killed Marcus at the first crime scene?'

'That's exactly what I'm thinking,' says John. 'The gunshot to Clive's head was so clean, so precise that I suspected he killed himself, though with guns it's hard to tell. Knives give much more of a clue.'

'But there is no knife here, and there was no gun at Marcus' place,' replies Liam.

All the while they've been talking, a thought begun in my head, then mutated and formed. Now, it's ready to be shared.

'Someone is making them do it,' I say, 'and then clearing up after them.'

The silence in the room is deafening.

11

ZOE'S PARENTS LIVE in Wilmslow, a well-to-do town about thirty minutes south of Manchester. Their house is on a cul-de-sac with a wide road, near to the town centre. Large semi-detached houses with sash windows and expensive cars loom over the street, each with a vast front garden blooming with colourful summer flowers.

We pull up on the kerb and survey the home in front of us. Lights flash through a gap in the curtains, which have been pulled over the living room window, indicating that, despite it being close to midnight, someone is awake. Liam opens the gate, which could do with a drop of oil, and we walk up the paved path towards the door. I knock lightly on the wood and a minute later, the heavy front door with coloured frosted glass, much like the windows in the church, opens.

The man in front of us must be around fifty years old, but looks much younger. Dark, tousled hair and vivid blue eyes—which seem to cast a light of their own—rake over Liam, then me. A well-maintained beard engulfs his lips and when he smiles, his teeth are almost as bright as his eyes. He is holding a small glass of pungent amber liquid.

'Mr Sullivan?' I venture.

'Can I help?' he asks with a hint of an Australian accent.

I flash my badge and his shoulders slump an inch or two. I ask if we could come in, and he agrees, apologising time and time again for his lack of manners. He leads us into the living room, the television showing a sport I don't know, though it seems like a form of rugby.

'Aussie Rules,' he explains, noticing my confused expression. He tells us to take a seat on the sofa and asks if he can get us a drink, which we decline. He seems to come to the conclusion that drinking alcohol in front of the police is somehow wrong, and puts the tumbler on the top shelf of a nearby bookcase, lined with old tomes and some contemporary fiction. He takes a seat on the other sofa, perpendicular to the one we are on, and turns the television off when he finds the remote control. He adjusts his position and those intense eyes fix upon us.

'Mr Sullivan…'

'Noel,' he says, warmly.

'Noel, I'm sorry to say that we have found the body of your daughter, Zoe, this evening,' says Liam.

He bristles slightly, but other than that he looks like a statue. He stares unblinking into the space between Liam and myself, before heaving a huge sigh, a rueful smile spreading across his face.

'At least she's finally at peace,' he says, his eyes filling with tears. I look at him inquisitively and he elaborates.

'Zoe has always been a troubled girl. The teachers at primary school used to be very worried about her. She was very moody and withdrawn, had almost no inclination to make friends. The kids would call her a loner and she was often bullied. Then, when she got a bit older, she started to self-harm. Little cuts on places she thought we wouldn't notice. Then, it started on the wrists. She was hospitalised twice; overdose the first time. Not enough to kill her, but enough to give us a good scare. The second time was worse. We found her lying in the bath, her left wrist was cut almost to the bone.'

He dabs at his eye, the memory jarring.

'Did Zoe live here?'

'No,' he replies. 'She lives in the city centre with a friend from work. Probably her only friend.'

'Do you have a name?'

'Eleanor Wilson. She is a lovely girl. We were concerned when Zoe said she was moving out to live in the city, but when we met

Ellie, our trepidation lessened. I can get you the address of their flat if you'd like?'

He gets up from the sofa and walks to an oak sideboard, pulls out a drawer. Sheets of paper erupt, threatening to spill over the sides. It's almost like a metaphor for Noel's life. Calm on the surface, a mess underneath. He lifts the papers and fishes in the bottom of the drawer, his tongue between his teeth, before pulling a tatty address book out. He leafs through it and, when he finds the page he needs, copies the address onto a luminous yellow post-it note.

'You said *we?*' I say, recalling the conversation about finding Zoe in the bath.

'My wife and I, Susanne. She's away on business at the minute, in Doha. She's going to be heartbroken.' His voice cracks and he buries his face in his hands.

Poor man. Having to cope with all of this alone tonight.

I give him a few minutes before reaching into my bag and showing him a picture of Kai McCormick, alive and well, pulled from his Facebook page.

'Do you recognise this man?' I ask him.

He shakes his head almost straight away. 'Should I?' he asks.

I steady myself. The man has been through so much. Now, I'm about to add to the trauma that he will have to carry with him the rest of his life.

'I'm afraid Zoe didn't just kill herself tonight, we believe she also killed this man.'

He lurches forward suddenly and covers his mouth with his hands. I worry he is going to be sick.

'We brought her up to be better than this,' he says, over and over again, until it almost sounds like a religious chant. I stand and walk towards him, placing a hand on his shoulder. This seems to calm him somewhat.

'I'm sorry, you must think she was dreadful.' He trails off again and begins to wail. 'She wasn't... she just wasn't well...'

'Mr Sullivan,' I say, after a time and he turns to face me, a defeated look in his eyes. 'We believe that she may have been told to. Perhaps, coerced into doing it. We don't know by who, or why, but you may be able to help us with that.'

He gives a little sniffle.

'Does the name Greg Webster mean anything to you?'

He shakes his head.

'What about Oliver Pilkington, sometimes known as Olly?'

'She dated an Olly a few years ago,' he says, his face visibly paling at the mention of the name. 'Nasty little man, as I recall. I implored Zoe to break up with him, but my pleading was probably the glue that held them together for two months longer. He was a few years older than her and I really was not a fan.'

Liam and I exchange a disbelieving look.

'Do you think he was the one who told her to kill?' he asks, through gritted teeth.

IT'S ALMOST HALF-PAST one in the morning when we turn into the estate where Kai's parent's live. A surprising number of windows have been boarded up—though, considering the area, perhaps it's not *that* surprising. Rusty cars without wheels, up on bricks, stand sentinel on the street.

We travel through the rabbit's warren until we reach the road containing their house. We pull up outside number eleven, a boxy council house with a broken gate which leads to a small, overgrown front garden. Loud, rhythmic music—the type usually heard in sweaty nightclubs in the Balearics—leaks through the single-glazed windows out onto the otherwise quiet street.

I gaze around at the other houses and notice that they are in darkness. Either the neighbours have battened down the hatches to try and get some sleep, or, judging by the multitude of silhouettes dancing behind the pulled curtains, have abandoned their own homes and the pursuit of sleep in favour of a drunken party with Kai McCormick's parents.

I knock on the door and when no one comes to answer, I cross the tiny patch of grass, which reaches my knee, and hammer on the kitchen window. The curtains flutter and are pulled back, a woman's face appearing in the crack. She squints into the darkness, notices me and nearly jumps out of her skin, before breaking into fits of laughter. She releases her hold on the curtains and a minute later, the door opens.

The same woman is standing in the doorway. Her blanched face is accentuated by vivid red lipstick. A tight, tie-dyed dress hugs her body and barely conceals her breasts.

'Gave me a fright, you did,' she squawks, pointing at me.

'Are you Mrs McCormick?' I ask.

She shakes her head, the wine in her hand sloshing over the top of her glass.

'I'll go and grab her for ya,' she says, leaving the door open and waltzing into the crowded living room.

A few minutes later, a nasty-looking man wearing a bucket hat and a grey T-shirt, stained with sweat under the armpits, appears. He attempts to study us with unfocussed eyes and, in the process, stumbles forward a few steps, before taking a seat on the front step.

I introduce myself and Liam, and this elicits an ill-tempered snigger.

'I suppose you want us to turn the music down. Has some snivelling twat called you about my birthday party?' he says, looking around the estate, as if searching for the alleged party-pooper.

Looking at his furrowed brow and his pock-marked face, I can't help but think that he may be one of the most unpleasant men I've ever met. And I've met a lot. He is clearly under the influence of alcohol, and looking at the track marks on the inside of his arms, possibly some very hefty, not to mention highly illegal, intravenous drugs. He probably has a rap sheet a mile long and there are doubtless hundreds of reasons we could arrest him, but I remind myself that this is not the reason we are here. We're here with devastating news.

'Mr McCormick, I'm not here to tell you to end your party. Though it is getting on a bit,' I add, unable to help myself.

He glowers at me from underneath his hat and takes a swig from his beer bottle. He sets the bottle down on the step with a scraping noise, then wipes the liquid off his stubbly chin with the back of his hand.

'If you aren't here for that,' he says. 'Why are you here?'

'Mr McCormick,' I say again, willing myself to be on his side, 'I'm afraid it's to do with your son.'

At the mention of his son, he grabs his bottle from the step and stands up, turning back to the door.

'Did you hear…?' I start, though I'm swiftly interrupted.

'Look, whatever that stupid fucker has done now,' he growls, looking back at us, 'I bet he brought it on himself. He's a nasty piece of work. I've given him the benefit of the doubt too many times and always had it thrown back in my face. He's nicked money from us. He broke my arm two years ago over a packet of cigarettes. And after the shit he pulled last time I saw him, well…'

'I'm afraid to tell you your son has been murdered,' I state, baldly.

He looks, for a moment, that the news will break through his wall of anger, but alas not.

'Like I said,' he says, with a little shrug of his shoulders, 'I bet he brought it on himself.'

He turns and, without another word, lets himself into the house, leaving Liam and I standing dumbfounded in his garden.

12

ROSS POWELL'S HAIRY stomach droops out from under his multi-coloured T-shirt, which features an array of mighty-looking comic book fighters, clad in metallic suits. His bald head glistens with perspiration from the effort of climbing a single set of stairs to get to the briefing room, which we are now standing outside of. The smell of stale sweat drifts out from under his armpits, the cotton of his T-shirt damp and stained. That trademark grin of his is plastered across his face.

'Remember,' I say to him. 'It's Bob's first day back at work, and he and Clive went way, way back. Don't go into anything unnecessary.'

He gives me a look that makes me feel like I'm being patronising, though he gives me a small nod anyway.

Ross has been part of the technological police team for many years, and has been instrumental in cracking many cases. What he doesn't know about computers isn't worth talking about.

He turns and walks into the briefing room. A tree has formed on the light blue material on the back of his top; sweaty branches reach out to the edges of the fabric. I follow him in and assume my place at the front of the room, while he throws himself heavily into a chair at the side. He places his laptop under his seat and leans back with a groan. I pull the case board into the centre of the room, its wheels squeaking as it goes. I look around the room and notice, not for the first time that, since Tom left, there aren't many of the old guard remaining.

Liam sits beside Angela, deep in conversation—the two remaining Detective Sergeants. Aside from me, a host of new-ish faces that have been recruited in the past six months look up at me with expectant eyes and an empty seat resides where DCI Bob should be. I wonder if he got cold feet about coming back.

Just as the thought crosses my mind, the door opens, and he slouches into the room. Since I last saw him, standing over the murdered body of his friend, he appears to have aged ten years.

'Not late, am I?' he asks.

I shake my head.

'Let's get it over with, then.'

On the case board are a number of pictures. Four faces, once alive but now no longer, peer out at us with varying expressions. Two more faces, those of Olly Pilkington and Greg Webster, join them, scowling at the assembled group from the far side of the board. A map, with two red circles indicating where the two murder-suicides took place, fills the middle space.

I point, first to Clive, and then to Marcus.

'On the night of Saturday, the third of August, we believe that Clive travelled from his home in Bury to Manchester, specifically to Bennett Street. Here, he gained entry to the home of Marcus Stone and shot him, before shooting himself.' I now point to Greg's face. 'Greg Webster, who we believe may be the one behind this, was captured on CCTV in the area around the time of the deaths, and given that Marcus had recently given his daughter a black eye, he has a motive as well. We also know that Clive and Greg had previous when Clive was working as a DI in Manchester. So, Greg may be the one doing the coercing.'

I now point to Zoe and then to Kai.

'Then, last night, the bodies of Zoe Sullivan and Kai McCormick were found dead in St. Peter & The Light church, across the street from where the first bodies were found. Evidence suggests that Zoe stabbed Kai to death, before turning the knife on herself. The similarities of the deaths and the gang link between Marcus and Kai are so far the only concrete leads we have.'

'Are we really thinking that this little girl,' Bob points a fat finger at Zoe's face, 'could overpower him?' He points to Kai.

I shuffle some of the paper on the desk behind the case board, searching for a folder. Eventually, I lay my hand on it and carefully pull out the two pieces of paper I need. I hold them out to the room, though the writing is much too small for anyone to see.

'This came through from John Kirrane. A tox report, taken during the autopsy of Marcus, suggests that he was drugged. The same cannot be said of the supposed killer. My guess is that the same will come back from the next two; Kai drugged, Zoe not. Couple this with the fact that no murder weapons have been found, and—'

'—you think that someone is organising this?' Bob interrupts.

'At the moment, it seems that way. The fact that the murder weapons have not been located suggests a third-party involvement. This is further backed up by what Ross has managed to find.'

I vacate the space at the front of the room, leaving it wide open for the computer expert. His chair groans beneath him as he gets up.

'Hi, everyone,' he says, sounding nervous.

He gives a small wave that reminds me of a child waving at their mother and father in the audience of a school play.

'I'll start with Clive. When Erika went to speak to his wife, she indicated that he was spending more time locked away in his office and was becoming very security conscious about his computer. Well, when we got in the lab, it was easy to see why. The guy was watching a lot of porn! And I mean a lo...'

He trails off when he catches my eye, the wide grin falling from his face as my words from earlier, *don't go into anything unnecessary,* crash around his head. I can only see the back of Bob's neck but, even from that, I can tell that his face must be a violent purple. Ross hurries along.

'Uh... anyway... I also found that he had visited a number of sites about suicide. I've given the list to Erika. One he had bookmarked, foolishly. It was an article about suicide sites on the dark web; normal stuff like forums where people discuss their feelings and whatnot. But there was the suggestion that the site had advice on how to do it too, ranked by pain levels and all sorts. Dark web activity is almost impossible to trace, but there is evidence to suggest that he did visit some of the suggested suicide pages.'

He walks across to the chair and picks up the laptop he had under his arm when he arrived.

'This is Zoe's,' he said, holding the laptop up. 'I only got it this morning and I've only had a brief look, but it's a similar story. She was less security conscious than Clive. At first, she shows a slight interest in regular suicide sites, before seemingly learning about the dark web's offerings. She then visited a number of sites about how to get on the dark web.'

He pulls a glum face.

'Like I say, I only got it this morning, but my hypothesis is that I imagine we will find a number of sites she has visited on the dark web. I also imagine that those will overlap with the ones Clive visited too. The way to find out who the puppeteer is, is to cross reference all the sites. Find out which one was the one that offered to help end their lives.'

Bob stands up. He looks viciously angry and sad at the same time.

'It's all very well finding out how to kill yourself and going through with it,' he barks. 'But what makes you want to take someone else's life at the same time?'

'That's exactly what we need to find out,' I reply.

THE LIVING ROOM of the vicarage where the Reverend Richard Clark lives is large, yet cosy. A sprawling teal corner sofa sits invitingly opposite the door, accessorised with oversized cream and red striped cushions. A bookcase filled with different versions of the Bible and other religious texts stands next to a sideboard, the top of which is neatly organised. Photographs in matching frames are spaced equidistant along the cream walls. A crucifix has been fixed above the fireplace.

Richard enters the room with a tray and places it softly on the table in front of us, the liquid in the mugs barely disturbed. He takes his own tea and leaves the tray with our mugs and a plate of biscuits in front of us. He crosses the room and sinks into a well-used rocking chair, placing his mug on a slate coaster on a table next to him. He moves a well-thumbed Bible and a pair of reading glasses from the table onto the floor.

'Thanks so much for seeing us, Mr Clark,' I say.

'Richard,' he replies, 'please, call me Richard.'

The dark rings under his eyes suggest that he has not had an easy night of sleep. I imagine after what he had seen, his head was filled with all kinds of unwanted images.

'Please can you run us through last night?'

He picks his mug up and takes a little sip, though he keeps it in his hands instead of placing it down again.

'Well, I was here writing my sermon for Sunday and I realised that I'd left some of my notes in the office in the church, where we met last night. I decided to nip across, it's only a ten-minute walk or so. The front doors were locked as they often are in the evening, but the side door wasn't. Again, this is nothing out of the ordinary. We often leave them open so that anyone who wants to access the church for prayer or reflection can get in. When I got there, well…'

He stops. His stare becomes far away and his eyes glass over. It's obvious what he is reliving.

'How come the front doors were open when we got there?' Liam asks, causing Richard to jump, startled out of his recollection.

'The police officer, the first one who got there, asked me to unlock them as the equipment they'd need to bring in was too wide for the side door.'

'Did you know either of the victims?' I ask.

'I did. Only the man, Kai. And I knew Marcus, the boy who was murdered a few days ago. I saw his pictures in the paper and, of course, heard all about it from the lads on the street.'

'How?'

'We've recently started a sort of... outreach, I suppose you would call it. The church is in quite a deprived area and the gang culture is tearing it apart. Myself and the assistant vicar, Jack, agreed that we needed to do something about it.'

He goes on to describe how they had agreed that the gang members might not feel comfortable coming into a church to be judged, so they had hit upon the idea. The idea was similar to confession, borrowed from the Catholic Church. They had set up a room in the church where anyone could come. The room was spilt in two by a dark curtain; the confessor would sit on one side and the unjudging listener would sit on the other. Whoever came didn't have to identify themselves.

At the start, he admits, it didn't really take off. One or two people came, introduced themselves as Mickey Mouse or Clark Kent, and generally took the piss. Gradually, a number of the younger members came and told him that they felt pressured into joining the gang and took advice on how to proceed. Then, higher ranking members came to confess their wrongdoings. Richard and his assistant were pleased with the progress they were and are making, though not everyone in the church was.

'Who was unhappy?' Liam asks.

'A number of the congregation and a few of the other people who work there, especially the caretaker,' he replies.

'Why?'

'Well, they verbalised their displeasure that we were letting evil into the church. Some of the lads who came admitted to causing bodily harm to others, drink driving and drug dealing. The caretaker came to me one night last week and reminded me about the flood in Genesis and the destruction of Sodom and Gomorrah. He said

God had a way of dealing with true sinners and that it wasn't to invite them into his house.'

'Who is this man?'

'His name is Ken Edwards.'

'How did you respond?' I ask.

'Well, initially I was very shocked. This is obviously a man who I trust to look after the church, though truth be told, we've had a slightly fractious relationship since I started. He is a very much in favour of the Old Testament style God—death and destruction to all sinners—whilst I am obviously much more in favour of a church filled with love and compassion, a church that is open to everyone.

Anyway, I reminded him of the parable Jesus told about the sinning woman at dinner who washed his feet and was absolved of her sins. Ken left, grumbling about being soft.'

I make a note in my pad to find out more about this Ken Edwards.

'Obviously,' Richard says, 'I don't believe he's got anything to do with this. As much as he doesn't agree with our outreach program, I'd never believe him to be capable of murder.'

I nod to show that I understand his point of view, before changing the angle of questioning.

'Do you know Olly Pilkington?'

'Not personally,' he says, 'but his name did come up during our sessions. Some of the lads hated him, most feared him. The impression I got of him was that he was a nasty piece of work. I'd love to spend some time with him, maybe get him into a session.'

And I'd love to win the lottery and retire to my own private island. That, I think to myself, has a higher probability of happening than Olly Pilkington ever stepping foot in Richard's church.

We get up from the sofa and thank him for his time. As we make our way to the door, Liam points at a picture of Richard and a woman with curly blonde hair arm in arm, looking down at the expansive streets of New York City from atop one of its many skyscrapers. Another beside it, in an identical frame, shows Richard and the same woman, except this time there is a small baby between them, sleeping soundly in a Moses Basket. It can't be more than a few weeks old.

'Is this your wife?' Liam asks.

'It is.'

'I didn't think vicars were allowed to get married.'

'You're thinking of Catholic priests. Sadly, Claire died at the start of last year in a car accident.'

'And...' Liam starts, though he is interrupted by Richard.

'Yes,' he says, tears springing to his eyes, 'the little light of my life, Izzy, died the same night. The doctors told me she wouldn't have suffered, which is a small blessing. All my life, I'd wanted to be a father. You see, my own father didn't treat me well. I was taken into foster care at an early age and I vowed that, if I were lucky enough to have a child, I'd give them everything they'd ever need. Unfortunately, I only had four months with my little Izz.'

I can feel the sting of tears in my own eyes and that horrible feeling in the nose when you try to fight them back. To not be able to conceive a child is a hard thing to live with. But to be given such a precious gift, and to have it taken away from you almost immediately in such devastating circumstances must be unbearable. I wipe my hand on my seeping nostril and turn back to him. We mumble our apologies, but he shakes his head.

'It hurt like hell,' he admits. 'It shook my faith in God and made me question if I wanted to continue with my ministry. I was so angry with everyone. How could such an awful thing happen to a good person? I prayed and prayed, and eventually God answered. I looked around our local area at the deprivation and vowed to use my hurt to try and make a change. In the book of John, Jesus said *In me ye might have peace. In the world ye shall have tribulation: but be of good cheer; I have overcome the world.* Those words gave me a sense of solace.'

He walks us to the door and bids us farewell with a little wave. When he closes the door, Liam and I make our way down his garden path and get into the car. It feels like a greenhouse in here.

'How fucked up is it to think that your wife dying is part of a plan?' Liam says, as he turns the key in the ignition.

'He didn't say it was part of a plan. He said he wanted to use the hurt to ignite a change. I think it's admirable.'

Liam scoffs. I know that as a church-goer from an early age, he was shocked by the reaction to his coming out. The church made him feel unwelcome in his teenage years, and his faith in God had all but disappeared. Couple that with a job where you witness first-hand what humanity is capable of, and I get his point. *Why would a loving God let things like that car crash happen?*

'I think I'd like another look around the church,' I say.

As Liam moves away from the kerb, my phone rings. I answer and listen to the information being passed to me in machine gun fire snippets, and a wry smile passes over my face as Angela finishes her spiel.

'The church will have to wait,' I say to Liam. 'Let's head to *Byte It*. It turns out that Greg Webster has been spotted on CCTV walking past the church last night, at roughly the same time as the murders are purported to have happened.'

13

BYTE IT IS a blink-and-you'd-miss-it shop in the middle of Manchester city centre, though calling the narrow strip of space a shop might seem like you are trying to take the piss. It's a glorified indoor alleyway.

Inside, on either side of the walkway, which is only about five feet long, are glass cases filled to the brim with computer parts. Although it all looks like a huge mess to me, Liam is beside himself with excitement. He scans the cases, pointing at various ancient games consoles and telling me about memories from his childhood; how his brother snapped one of the cartridges inside a SNES, whatever that is, and the time he got a MegaDrive for Christmas but his parents forgot to buy him any games so it was useless until the shops opened again. Neither sound like good memories to me. All I can think of when I look at the tat inside the cases is how many germs there must be all over the joysticks. God, am I getting old?

A man in his mid-forties with spiky hair and a carefully maintained beard emerges from the door at the back of the shop. He welcomes us and immediately latches on to Liam's enthusiasm for the shop's wares. The two have a few minutes of back and forth about things I don't understand.

'What brings you here today?' he asks, once the excitement levels have abated slightly. 'Are you looking for anything in particular?'

'I'm DI Erika Piper and this is DS Liam Sutton. Are you the manager?'

He confirms that he is, and introduces himself as Paul Day.

'We're wanting to talk to one of your employees, a Greg Webster.'

'Ha, well, if you manage to find him, tell him I'd like a word too. This is the second day in a row he's messed me about. Yesterday, he left at lunch and didn't come back. Today, no sign at all. No answer on his phone or anything.'

I consider this information.

'How long has he been working here?' I ask.

He takes a moment.

'We started working with him when he was in prison, one of our apprentice schemes, I guess you'd call it. When he was released just over a year ago, he came to work here full time.'

'So you've known him quite a long time?'

'Almost three years.'

'Has he been a good addition to your business?' Liam asks.

'Absolutely,' he nods.

'You didn't have any worries about taking on someone you met in prison?'

'Not at all. I like to think I'm a good judge of character and I believe in second chances, especially when it is clear that the rehabilitation process has worked.'

A phone rings in the back room and he excuses himself politely. Liam turns his back and checks the stock in the other case while I try and get a look through the glass in the door that separates us from the back room. In less than a minute, Paul is back behind the counter, muttering apologies to us. I pick up the line of questioning.

'Is this little AWOL stunt out of the ordinary for him?'

'I've never had any issues with him before yesterday. I've heard him get annoyed at printers in the back room, but who hasn't got angry at one of those before? They're sent from the devil himself.' He chuckles at his own joke. 'No, he's always been courteous to customers, both face to face and on the phone. He's never been late and he's never done anything to warrant any suspicion.'

So, what's changed in the past few days I wonder to myself.

'Did he give a reason for leaving yesterday?' I ask.

'No. He seemed to be in a bad mood in the morning. He was pretty quiet. Then, when he left for lunch, he didn't say anything. He just left and never came back. When I phoned him, it just rang out.'

'And he didn't give any indication about why he was moody?'

He shakes his head. 'He's not in trouble, is he?'

I can neither confirm, nor deny, as I do not know myself. Before we leave, Paul gives us Greg's home address and tries to persuade Liam into buying one of the consoles. I drag him out of the shop before he has time to locate his wallet.

GREG'S POST-PRISON accommodation is not a pretty picture. A high-rise block, similar to the one his daughter lives in, looms above us. If anything, it's less inviting than Kylie's place of residence. And that is saying something. I imagine for someone trying to kick an almost lifelong drug and alcohol addiction, this area does him no favours. The smell of weed hits me the moment I leave the car.

I look in the window of the ground-floor flat that I've been told belongs to Greg. A two-seater leather sofa faces a wooden cabinet, upon which a small flatscreen television sits. The remaining furniture is mismatched, both in colour and size, and the place feels like it has been furnished using one of those freecycle websites. A take what you can get kind of job. There doesn't seem to be a mirror or any of the other little touches that make a house feel like a home, though it does look clean and tidy.

The other window belongs to the kitchen. A pretty tidy kitchen at that. Utensils are held upright in a ceramic pot by the hob. A pair of oven gloves hang limp over the handle of the oven door. Clean pots, pans and plates rest in a dish drainer by the side of the sink. There is no sign of any fermenting ready meal boxes or rotting week-old takeaway leftovers. Part of me wonders if we have the right house.

I knock on the door and wait for a few minutes before repeating the rhythmic pattern, but there is no answer. A narrow alleyway at the side of the flat leads to a wooden gate, which I imagine opens up into some form of communal space and Greg's back door. I walk down the graffitied alley and stop at the shoddily built gate. Rusty nail ends protrude through the wood, and I worry I'll need a tetanus if I accidentally scrape one of them with my hand. I give the gate a shake, that does nothing.

It's then that I notice the latch at shoulder level, and just as I am about to push it up, the gate is pulled open from the inside and Greg comes storming out of the opening. Something glints in his hand. I retreat down the alley and into the open space near our car. Greg comes stumbling out of the alley, with a broken shard of a vodka bottle raised above his head. He fixes me with a bleary-eyed look.

'It's you,' he shouts.

He's wearing a red T-shirt with the *Byte It* logo embroidered onto the left side of the chest. The knees of his jeans are stained with dirt and he's missing a shoe. I try to reason with him; tell him to let go of the razor-sharp glass in his hand. He looks slowly from me to the glass like it's the first time he's seen it, before throwing it onto the tarmac, where it smashes into hundreds of tiny fragments.

'Officers,' he slurs. 'I've done something silly.'

He begins to cry as we lead him willingly to the police car.

WE GIVE HIM a few hours in the drunk tank before hauling him into the interview room. His speech is much less slurred now, though the stench of alcohol coming across the table is enough to make me move my chair back. I check my watch to find that the day is passing us by—it's almost four o'clock already and I realise that in all the excitement the day has brought us, I've forgotten to eat.

'How are you feeling?' I ask.

'A lot better, thank you,' he says, raising his cup of water in our direction.

'Greg, I'm going to be straight with you. The reason we came to your house today is that you were caught on CCTV outside St. Peter & The Light shortly before two bodies were discovered inside. Can you shed some light on that for us?'

He looks at me with a very confused look upon his face.

'Bodies?'

'Two of them,' I confirm. 'Can you explain what you were doing in the area?'

'Yes,' he nods. 'I was getting the 142 bus home after work, like I always do. I thought I'd jump off a bit early and go to see Kylie, check how she was doing after what happened the other night. That's why I got off the bus near the church. It's only a ten-minute walk from there to her place. When I got off, I phoned her to let her know I was on my way, but she told me she was heading to the cinema with a friend.'

'We know that you weren't at work all day,' says Liam.

He looks like a little boy who has been caught out.

'That's what I was talking about when I said to you earlier that I'd done something silly.' He looks at me. 'I went to the pub for lunch and had a beer. The stress of the last few days; the black eye, Marcus being murdered, getting involved with the police again. It's all taken its toll. One thing leads to another and by the time I realised, I'd had a few, and I forgot all about work. When I couldn't go to see Kylie, I went to another pub on my way home and then to the offie where I got that bottle of vodka. I don't remember much after that.'

'So, the stupid thing you did was go back to drinking alcohol?'

'I've not had a drop in almost a year. I also lost my keys and had to sleep in the garden. My phone ran out of battery so I couldn't set an alarm to get up for work.' His eyes begin to water. 'I bet I'm going to get fired.'

I think I believe him. He genuinely does seem like a changed man. Before now, remorse has never been his strong suit.

'I'll put in a good word with your boss,' I say, and Liam shoots me a sideways glance. 'But I'm going to need something from you.'

'Anything,' he says.

'I'm going to need you to bring in your laptop.'

14

IT FEELS LIKE it's been one of those days where we have been on the go constantly, and despite Liam's protestations about there being no real need to be at the church today, we arrive on Bennett Street. We enter through the same gate I used last night, but instead of using the main doors, we walk on the paved path around the side of the church. The afternoon sun sits high in the cloudless blue sky, blasting us with its rays. Colourful summer flowers planted in hanging baskets release a sweet, sickly smell. A white metal sign with black embossed letters has been pushed into the grass, telling visitors that the grounds are maintained by church volunteers and to be considerate of their hard work by not walking on the grass or in the flowerbeds. Some of the letters are rusting and gravity has pulled thin iron trails towards the earth.

Around the side of the church is a small car park, big enough for about twenty cars but certainly not big enough to fit the entire congregation. Arlington Street runs parallel to Bennett Street, and it's from the Arlington side of the street that the car park is accessible. A heavy wooden gate has been tethered to a concrete post, allowing free entry.

Currently, only one car is making use of the car park. It is a dark green estate car with an 02 number plate, making it nearly twenty years old. It has seen better days. On first glance, I can see that rust has accumulated around the wheel arches, the windscreen has a small crack in it, and a number of little dents line the driver's side doors.

The square car park narrows into an alleyway which stretches behind the church building, linking it to the opposite side of the church grounds. A number of bins narrow the entrance to the alley further, though they spark a little grain of excitement in me.

'Forensics checked the bins for the murder weapon. No dice. Turns out we're not dealing with an absolute dummy here, sadly,' Liam says from behind me, noticing the spring in my step.

My excitement is gone.

Aside from some stunning stained-glass windows and a few weeds poking through the paving slabs below our feet, there isn't much to see. A low wall, separating the car park from the alleyway, is covered in graffiti. Faded paint professes attraction, offers phone numbers and arranges fights. Memories of love, hate and hope.

A door with a black metal handle; similar to the front door of the church, though not as tall and half as wide, is sunk a few feet into a little alcove. I give the handle a pull and, though it judders slightly in its frame, it doesn't open. I reckon that this is the door that was being blocked by Zoe's lifeless body. I shine my torch on the surrounding frame and brick work, but there doesn't seem to be any sign of forced entry. Considering what Richard said about the door being left open, this makes sense. It also makes sense that it has been locked today, in view of what happened last night.

Surveying the upper area of the church, and, despite a sign warning car park users that CCTV is in operation and that their vehicles are left here at their own risk, no actual cameras are evident. I walk back down the alley and check around the corner from where we came. Again, no camera. Looking out onto Arlington Street, I can only see one, hanging uselessly from the top of a lamppost, long taken care of by the local lads I'd imagine.

As we are about to walk back down the alley and round to the other side of the church, the door bursts open. Despite the sun, not much light makes it into the alley, and my hand instinctively reaches for my gun. A man with thick grey hair which is combed to the side and a broken-at-least-twice nose appears in the doorway. A sculpted moustache hugs his top lip. He peers out into the alley and when he sees us, recoils back, startled.

'What are you doing back here?' he barks in a long-softened Scottish accent.

I walk towards him, holding my police ID aloft. He steps closer to take a look, a waft of Old Spice filling the gap between us.

'You gave me a fright,' he says, setting the bin bags down and giving his brow a mop with a monogrammed handkerchief.

'Sorry about that,' I reply as he stuffs the hankie back into the front pocket of his blue overalls, picks up the overflowing bags and hoists them into the bins with ease. He rubs his nose again as he approaches us and asks us if we'd like to come in.

'KENNETH, OR KEN to my friends,' he says, shaking our hands as we take a seat in a room near the front entrance of the church.

Kenneth, or Ken to his friends, is knocking on seventy years old, though is surprisingly limber considering the ease with which he dealt with the bin bags.

'Can you tell us anything about last night, Ken?' Liam asks, pulling his notebook out of his pocket.

'Not much you probably don't already know. I did the bits and pieces I needed to get done in the day. I volunteer here as a caretaker, you see. Anyway, when I was done, I went home. I only live up the road. I usually bob back down around ten o'clock but I got a call from Dick…'

'Richard?'

He looks a little embarrassed. 'Aye, Richard. I got a call from him telling me that I wouldn't be needed. That there was an incident at the church and to stay away.'

'What time was this?' I ask.

'About…' he pauses; looks up. 'It was just as the second Corrie was starting, so about half-eight I reckon.'

'Richard told us you weren't a fan of his and,' I check my notes, 'Jack's outreach idea.'

His cheeks suddenly flush a vivid red.

'You're damn right I'm not a fan,' he says, using air quotes for the last three words. Some spittle has collected in his moustache.

'Why?'

'Because I believe the church building should be used solely for people wanting to worship God. I don't mind what he is doing, but I'd rather he did it elsewhere.'

'He says crime is down in the area.'

'Ha,' he snorts, pulling the handkerchief back out of his pocket and wiping his nose again. 'I'd argue against that opinion with four dead bodies found this week within a stone's throw of each other.'

The man has a point.

'Isn't that the whole point of church? To help sinners?' Liam asks.

'It is,' Ken nods. 'Look, I see what he is trying to do, and I do think his heart is in the right place, but these lads are beyond saving. Drug dealers, joyriders and thieves—unrepentant, all—have no place in God's house. I think Richard is soft, and playing with fire.'

I get the feeling that Kenneth has never backed down from an argument in his life. It's the strong constitution I'd expect from a fiery, old Scot. I fix him with my hardest stare and ask him the sixty-four-thousand-dollar question.

'Do you believe that they deserved to die?'

He takes a moment to consider my rather up-front question.

'I do,' he replies, nodding his head. He looks me in the eye, unblinking. 'God preached an eye for an eye, and I fully agree with my Lord and Saviour.'

'Did you have anything to do with it?' Liam asks.

This time he answers quickly. A resounding no.

We thank Kenneth for his time and leave the room, meaning to have a look around, though he follows us out and, intentionally or not, ushers us towards the door, mumbling about how it's time to lock up.

'Is that yours?' I ask, pointing at the green car.

'No,' he laughs. 'That monstrosity belongs to Richard. He often parks here when he is doing his rounds on the streets. I've not been allowed to drive for a few years now, on account of my failing vision.'

He closes the door behind us all with a bang, and a small click signifies that it has been locked. He bids us farewell, before walking off towards Bennett Street, whistling as he goes.

15

9:00 PM. I do a double take of the clock mounted above the kitchen table. How in God's name is it only nine o'clock?

I've worked long days and even longer nights for years, and I've never felt as tired as I do today. I push the laptop away from me and pull my phone from my pocket. I fight an internal battle with myself, before pulling up the list of pregnancy symptoms again, feeling that I'm betraying myself in the process.

Fatigue. Check.

Nausea. Check.

Tender breasts. Now that I think of it, check. And, ouch.

A hat-trick.

But even with three from the list, I can feel the humiliation burning on my cheeks. Humiliation that my body is working against my brain, trying to trick it into thinking that the improbable, nay the impossible, is achievable.

My brain, now buoyed by the broodiness my body is experiencing, throws pictures in front of my eyes. I see me, in a hospital, cradling a bundle of cloth, a small life within. Me, leaning over a Moses basket, staring endlessly at a tiny baby, swaddled in blankets, chest rising and falling rhythmically. Me, clutching the baby to my chest, whispering in its ear that I will never let anything bad happen to it. The Moses Basket with Richard's now-deceased baby pops into my head and I feel my heart hammer that little bit faster.

The images come, and then go just as quickly. I wipe a tear away from my eye and pull the laptop towards me. Bury myself in work. Except, I can't, because the battery is about to die. I go to the cabinet, but the charger isn't there. Cursing, I check the drawers above and it isn't there either. Then, I remember that Tom had been using it upstairs last night. With an annoyed groan, I push myself away from the table and wearily ascend the stairs.

I push the door to the bedroom open and something falls off the hook on the back. I turn the light on and spot the charger, still plugged into the socket next to Tom's side of the bed. I retrieve it and check what fell on the floor. It's Tom's jacket, the lightweight one he was wearing in the restaurant last night before I was called away. A number of things have fallen out of the pocket; a few pennies, some of which have rolled under the bed, a dog-eared reward card for the Italian restaurant and, shockingly, a rectangular cardboard box with pink edging—which turns out to be a pregnancy test when I pick it up.

In the aftermath of my negative test, I remember him telling me about his sister taking the test too early. When I'd looked into it, an early test often fails due to a lack of hCG, a hormone only released when *with child*, to quote the very scientific article. I thought that story about his sister was just his way of trying to level his own disappointment, but it turns out it probably was true. I look down at the packet again and for a split second, I'm furious with him.

It's an open and shut case. I can't get pregnant. He shouldn't be making me confront that fact over and over again.

Then I thaw.

He didn't give me it. He didn't make me do it. He didn't even mention he had it. He could've bought it before I did mine; simply a relic of hope.

I'm about to toss it in the bin, but it's already overflowing. I decide to take it to the downstairs bin instead.

As I get to the top of the stairs, I stop. I think back to the trio of symptoms and a little bit of hope burns deep inside me. Foolish hope. In a parallel universe, I toss the hope aside, walk down the stairs and put the test in the bin.

But not in this universe.

A little hope will carry us home, sang a band my sister used to like. Hope is what separates us from animals. It can ridicule us and put us in jeopardy. But it can also be a little whisper that says *maybe*, when the whole word is shouting no.

I turn from the top of the stairs and go into the bathroom, closing the door behind me. I open the box and pull out the stick. I make a promise to myself that if the outcome is negative, which it 99.99% will be, that this is the last time I put myself through this, before pulling down my pants and doing the business.

Once complete, I set the stick on the edge of the bath, display side down so that I cannot see the outcome. I check the instructions, more out of something to do, than to know what to look for. They're all the same. My heart is hammering and I can already feel tears of resignation in my eyes. I feel foolish. If Tom asks about the test, I'll tell him I threw it away without opening it.

After a few minutes, which seem to stretch out before me like a long road reaching out into a very dark future, I take a tentative step towards the test and reach out, before stopping. An onlooker may think I have been scalded by an invisible something, or that I am taking part in some form of interpretive mime or dance. But I'm not. I simply stop because I can't bring myself to deal with the consequences of what this moment will bring.

Drawing on all the courage left in me, I reach for the stick and turn it over.

One blue line shows the test has worked.

One blue line, slightly fainter than its twin, tells me that there is improbable, implausible, beautiful life inside me.

16

TOM FOUND ME collapsed against the door, beaming and sobbing at the same time. It's been three days since the positive test and it feels like, for most of the time, my feet haven't touched the ground. Every morning I have woken up to Tom stroking my stomach, as if trying to pass as much love and luck into my womb as possible.

Small doubts have persisted in that time, too. Surely, the test must be mistaken. Or Tom bought a comedy test in order to trick me. Or he bought a legitimate test and it was faulty on its own accord. Thankfully, those doubts only amount to the 'visible-by-passing-ship' part of the iceberg, whilst the happiness is the huge mass below the surface of the ocean.

We decided we'd wait until the scan to tell people. Luckily, because of the circumstances, the hospital was very accommodating and the appointment is later today. Before that, computer whizz Ross Powell is due to come into the office and give us the lowdown on what he has managed to find out.

The case has moved at a glacial pace. So far, neither of the crime scenes has yielded any useful evidence, and the only thing holding it together is the list of websites visited by both murderers. Almost tenuous.

I pull the list of websites that Clive and Zoe visited and set them side by side. I look again at the highlighted websites, visited on both the normal web, and the dark web. The highlighted websites show the sites that both killers accessed in the time leading up to their deaths.

I am still working through the list of authentic websites—those not on the dark web. Most of the sites I've clicked on so far have either been self-help websites like Samaritans—those trying to talk you out of hurting yourself—or personal blogs of people considering suicide. It's made for insightful reading.

A number of the bloggers detail their feelings of sadness, loneliness and anger. How these emotions were pushing them to self-harm; first, little cuts in places no-one would notice and how those cuts escalated, ending in hospital visits. Some of the entries posted on the various blogs detail their rise out of depression, thanking a range of helpful entities. Some thank family for recognising the symptoms before they went too far; some thank TASC and PAPYRUS, organisations dealing with suicide prevention. Some of the blogs have not been updated in a while, which might signify that their fight with depression and anxiety, sadly, did not end well.

I get a pen and tick off the last few websites on the list, before retrieving the pages listing the websites found on the dark web. I close down my desktop and get the laptop Ross has prepared for me from under the desk, along with his instructions.

I open the laptop lid and type in the username he has sorted out for me, one that does not in any way associate me with my police work. He told me that an inexperienced dark web user, like myself, could have any amount of data taken from my computer and I wouldn't even know. I chose not to be offended by him calling me inexperienced.

The laptop he has provided for me has been factory reset, and the only thing on the home screen is the link for the Tor browser, my portal into the dark web. Black masking tape has been stuck over the webcam to bamboozle any would-be spies and the microphone has been removed. He joked, when handing the laptop to me, that it had been fool-proofed. Again, no offence taken.

I consult the list, narrowed down to four websites that both Clive and Zoe visited, and feel a chill run down my spine at their names; Take The Plunge, Welcome To The End, My Time To Die and Your Demise. I'm both struck and saddened by two things. One; the low ebb that someone must be feeling to bring themselves to visit websites such as these and, two; the sick lowlifes behind the websites who prey on the vulnerable under the guise of 'assistance.'

I open the Tor browser, renowned for its onion-skin like properties, layered with many levels of security, and key in the digits that will take me to the first of the pages—Take The Plunge.

The page loads and shows a smiling cartoon man with weights tied to his feet, standing on a bridge overlooking choppy waters. The frivolity of the image belies the darkness the site holds. I navigate to the forums. Some discuss how users of the site are feeling, some are a goodbye area—users so resigned to their fate that they have left a suicide note to faceless strangers that they once found a kinship with. The darker areas of the website detail methods for suicide and rankings, both of the pain they will cause and their effectiveness.

I scan through the forums for a while, hoping that a username like CLIVE1234 or ZoeSull will jump out. But people aren't that stupid, even when all hope of living has abandoned them. Though the website is undoubtedly ill-judged and most definitely illegal, none of the forums contain directives to kill another person. I put a cross beside the website's name and, as I'm about to move onto the next, there is a knock on my office door.

Ross Powell walks in, pulling handfuls of meat flavoured crisps greedily from a share size bag and stuffing them into his mouth. He stands in the doorway wearing an Iron Maiden T-shirt that is slightly too small for him and with crisp fragments in his beard, looking very much like that ginger dwarf from Lord of the Rings.

'How's it going on the websites?' he asks with a full mouth.

'Slowly,' I reply. 'I've just started on the dark web.'

'Ah, well, if you're going to find anything relating to the case it's going to be there,' he says, licking the flavouring off his fingers. 'I don't understand why you didn't start with those. A killer who doesn't want to get his hands dirty isn't going to be using Google.'

I nod, agreeing with him, whilst knowing that good police work means eliminating the obvious.

'You want some good news?' he asks, to which I nod again. 'Well, I searched Greg's computer like you asked. It didn't take too long to rule him out. In my humble opinion, he's not your man.'

I sigh. Ross's news is obviously good, but also frustrating because now our only lead is Olly Pilkington. Or maybe Kenneth, at a stretch.

'And Olly?'

He laughs. 'Olly didn't let us in. Told us he had nothing to do with it and to fu… well, to go away.'

'Can you look at his computer remotely?'

'Easily,' he nods. 'Though I'd need your permission.'

'You've got it,' I reply. 'I'll get you the warrant later today, but get started as soon as you can.'

'Thank you. Well,' he says, opening a folder containing pages of screenshots and other information, 'I've had a look and…'

'You mean you've already done it?'

'Yeah,' he shrugs, nonchalantly.

'What about my permission?'

'I knew you'd give it.'

'And if I hadn't?' I ask with a hint of a smile.

He smiles back. 'I'm clever enough to hide what I've done! Anyway, there is evidence on Olly's computer that he has been using the dark web. As of now, I've only found traces of him using websites concerning drugs. That's not to say he isn't using others, I just haven't dug deep enough yet.'

'Can you find out?'

'Of course,' he puffs out his chest, 'I just didn't want to go *too* far without your permission. I'll have a play around and see what I can find.'

He gives me a little wave as he leaves. Though Ross is no longer in the room, the smell of his BBQ beef crisps lingers; making me feel nauseous and when I check the time, I realise I've spent so much time researching the websites that I'm going to be late for my hospital appointment if I don't hustle. I close down the laptop, taking care to log out of the browser, grab my bag and rush out of the room.

THE WALLS OF the waiting room in the maternity unit of Stepping Hill hospital are covered in posters, promoting a healthy lifestyle and highlighting the problems smoking and drinking alcohol can pose whilst pregnant.

A TV screen shows a cartoon baby growing in size, week by week, inside its mother's womb. Bizarrely, as it grows, it is compared in size to a piece of fruit; beginning with a poppy seed at week one and culminating in a watermelon at week forty. The thought of squeezing a watermelon out of my body is making me feel queasy, so I avert my gaze from the tropical fruit.

Instead, I look around the room, sizing up the women here for the same reason as me. Some sit reading a magazine like this is all the most normal thing in the world, while some wait with worried looks on their faces. I imagine I am in the latter camp. Tom drapes a sweaty palm on my knee and I don't have the heart to move it. I know how he's feeling.

A short while later, my stomach somersaults as my name is called. I follow a young sonographer, who introduces herself as Matilda, into one of the rooms off the corridor. Matilda, in a very quiet voice, instructs me to lie down on the couch and to undo the button on my jeans. I do as I'm told and whilst she is getting herself ready, I take in the surroundings. Various glowing screens, beeping machines and medical implements on clinically clean metal tables surround me.

Matilda pulls on a pair of gloves, gives me a warm smile and squirts cold gel over my exposed belly. She dims the lights and turns off all but one of the screens, the remaining one casting a green-ish hue over the room. She pulls a probe from a hook attached to the table, coats the roller with more gel and places it softly on my stomach, almost apologetically. She runs it over my torso, pressing buttons on the keyboard, which changes what is displayed on the screen. She applies a bit more pressure, and I can see a momentary worried look flash across her face.

'Is everything OK?' Tom asks, making me jump. I'd almost forgotten he was there.

'I just need to speak to a colleague,' she says, smiling kindly again. She sets her equipment on the table and leaves the room, leaving us in a silence only punctuated by my sobs. I know what is happening. She can't find a heartbeat. I've seen this on Marley and Me.

Tom grasps for my hand and interlocks his fingers between mine. He rubs my heaving shoulder with the other hand. The terror of being told that this miracle is actually a mistake is coursing through my veins and causing my heart to hammer hard against my ribs.

The door opens with a click and an older woman enters with Matilda in her wake. She sits down on the stool and picks up the probe.

'Hi, I'm Annie,' she says, 'let's have a look at your baby.'

She either doesn't seem to notice my tears or else she is ignoring them. Matilda stands behind me, somewhere in the darkness.

The coldness spreads around my stomach again. I watch the screen as the empty chasm that is my womb is explored from different angles. I whimper an apology for the heaving of my stomach and try to control myself. She pulls the lead on the probe and presses it further to the left of my bellybutton.

And all of a sudden, a heartbeat fills the room. It booms out of the speakers and it is the sweetest sound I have ever heard. A look of relief spreads across Annie's face and she freezes the screen.

'See this?' she asks, pointing to a little black and white mass in the centre of the screen. 'This is your baby.'

I cry harder than I've ever cried.

17

'COULDN'T THIS HAVE waited until another night?' I ask Tom, as we pull into the car park of The Brookside Mill. Having got home after our appointment at the hospital earlier, I'd been looking forward to celebrating with a night in. Just the two of us. But Tom had insisted.

'Imagine your sister hadn't told you straight away when she found out she was pregnant. How would you have felt?' he asks as he pockets his keys.

I don't say anything because I know he is right, and he knows I know he is right. There is no need to verbalise it. Before we left, I'd also put forward the argument that a night away from the case was coming at the worst time. I could've been using the time to pore over notes and continue my needle-in-a-haystack search on the dark web. Again, he'd silenced me with a look and told me very calmly that I need to re-consider my priorities. Again, I knew he was right.

We get out of the car and he pushes open one of the double doors, ushering me inside before following. The smell of garlic and the sizzling sound of frying meat from the open kitchen welcome us. A waiter greets us just inside the door and leads us to a table near the back of the restaurant. My dad and sister, as well as Tom's mum and dad, are already seated. It's the first time they've all met, but they seem to be getting along well. The empty glasses in the middle of the table, alongside the half-filled ones currently in hand, may go some way to explaining that.

When we emerge from the archway, they stand up to greet us. Tom shakes hands with his dad and gives his mum a hug, while I latch on to dad and Sarah. Since mum died last year, each time I have seen dad he has looked like he is aging in fast forward. What little hair he had seemed to be retreating into his scalp and the weight of the world appeared to be pushing down on him, causing him to stoop over. It's been a few weeks since I've seen him, but tonight he looks well. His cheeks are fatter and his shirt and chino-style trousers don't dwarf him like they did a month ago.

'It looks like the move has treated you well,' I say to him, and he pulls a mock-offended face.

'What are you trying to say?' he gasps, theatrically, to much laughter from the table.

Just over a month ago, dad moved from the house he'd shared with mum for over thirty years to a bungalow near to where my sister lives. He claims that being close to Sophie, my sister's baby, has given him the drive to enjoy life again. And it shows. He seems happier. Healthier.

'Sorry that Will couldn't be here,' Sarah says, referring to her husband. 'We couldn't get a babysitter at such short notice.'

I wave her apology away just as the waiter comes and takes our drinks orders. When I order a diet coke, Sarah throws me a questioning look that I pretend not to notice. When he leaves, we descend into small talk. Sarah tells me about my niece's development; the horror of weaning, the poos that go along with the switch from milk to mush, and how cute her little gurgling noises are. A different waiter returns with our drinks and leaves with our food orders, which he tapped into a tablet, much to the bemusement of Tom's mother. She mumbles to Tom that she'll be very surprised if the food arrives as ordered. Tom's dad calls her a luddite.

'So,' Sarah says, 'what is all this in aid of?'

Silence befalls the table and all eyes move towards Tom and me. A smile reaches Tom's eyes.

'Well,' he says, taking a sip of his water, 'we have some news. And we couldn't wait to tell you.'

'Ohmygod,' Sarah interjects, 'you're getting married.' Her eyes rake over my hands, though, of course, there is no ring to be found. Tom shakes his head.

'We're not getting married,' I say, 'but we *are* having a baby.'

There is silence as the news is absorbed. Blank faces turn confused. Both sides of the family are well aware of my pregnancy woes, and they appear disbelieving at best. When I hold up a picture of the scan, chaos reigns. Tom's dad jumps up and pulls Tom into a bear hug. His mum is sobbing into her napkin. Sarah shrieks so loudly that the young couple at the table behind us jump in unison, throwing soup from spoons that were travelling to their open mouths into the air. Gravity makes a Jackson Pollock of their carefully chosen first date outfits.

'Stupid bitch,' the man mutters in Sarah's direction, as his dining companion scuttles off to the toilet.

Amongst the pandemonium, dad has remained still. His eyes are fixed on the little black-and-white picture in my hand. A single tear runs down his cheek. He stands up slowly and pulls me into a tight embrace.

'Your mother would be over the moon,' he says, and tears spring into my eyes. 'I'm so pleased for you, love.'

He releases me and wipes the tears from my face. The tenderness of the moment is broken as Sarah all but rugby tackles me and attacks me with questions that I don't yet have answers to. *Will our baby and Sophie be best friends? Will we find out what sex the baby is at our next scan? What school will it go to?*

When we retake our seats and the atmosphere calms, Tom's dad addresses Sarah. 'If you thought this tight bastard would pay for a wedding,' he jabs a thumb in his son's direction, 'you don't know him very well.' Cue more raucous laughter.

The night continues in this vein, only once brought down from its high spirits by a discussion about my job. Tom tells the table that after what happened in the mill—where he was almost killed—being a detective lost all of its appeal. Sarah asks if I'm going to give it up when the baby comes along, and Tom suggests I should give it up long before that. It's a discussion we've not had, and it's a consideration I've not given much thought to personally. The conversation moves on and when the bill has been paid, we move on to a nearby pub. The drinks flow and before I know it, it's past midnight. The enormity of the day hits me, and as I'm about to tell Tom that I'm ready for my bed, my phone rings.

'Hello,' I say, poking a finger into the other ear to try and cut out some of the noise as I walk towards the pub's door. I shiver as the coolness of the night hits me. I take a seat on a bench just outside the front door.

'Sorry to disturb you in the middle of the night,' a voice says, 'only I have someone on the line for you.'

'Who is it?' I ask.

'Her name is Manon Marchand. Shall I put you through?'

'Please.'

The calm voice of Stuart on reception is replaced with the frenetic voice of Manon. The wind howling down the phone tells me that she must be outside, as she is shouting to try and be heard above the gale.

'Can you hear me?' she yells, her French accent missing off the h of hear.

I tell her I can.

'I've killed someone, Detective. And I'm supposed to kill myself next, only I can't bring myself to do it.'

'Where are you?' I ask. Again, she screams above the noise of the wind, but I just about make out her location.

'Stay there,' I tell her, standing up and moving back towards the pub. 'I'll be right there.'

'I only want to speak to you,' she says, before hanging up.

ON ONE SIDE of the bridge, the famous Hat Works tower juts into the night sky, its outline and white lettering visible against the sea of stars. A small theatre underneath the tower has left a solitary light on in an upstairs window. On the other side of the bridge, a high-rise chain hotel is being bothered by off-key karaoke, which is escaping through the doors of a pub on the corner of the road, known for its rowdiness.

Behind us, across the normally busy A6, lies the glass facade of Stockport's shopping centre—The Merseyway. A security guard sits by the door on a stool, head drooping, possibly asleep on the job.

'This could be the break in the case we need,' says Liam, as he pulls up on the side of the road. There are other police cars and two forensics vans parked nearby, though none have approached the bridge so far, under my direction. Manon needs to trust the police and, if she only wants to speak to me, that's what we need to make happen. Liam and I cross the road and peer over the bridge. Though I can't see anything, I can hear sobbing. She is still where she said she was.

'Do you want me to come too?' asks Liam.

'No. Move over there.' I point to the left side of the bridge. 'You should be able to see what's happening from there and there are steps for quick access in case I do need you.'

He nods and walks to the spot I pointed out. He has a look and points his finger under the bridge, then taps his watch. I walk to the opposite side of the bridge and use the steps to access the area under the bridge.

The full moon is trying its best to light the area under the bridge for me, but the stone arches block most of it. It is a small metal square, built into the side of the bridge, possibly as a maintenance feature. A humming electrical box with an ironic 'Danger of Death' sticker is fixed into the corner.

Police officers have accessed the area frequently to move on homeless people who have started a fire in the middle of the night in an effort to keep warm. Tonight, the action playing out on the small square is far more sinister. A black mass hangs over the dark river, suspended from one of the railings by a noose. The thick rope has been expertly knotted and is about six foot long. At the end of the rope is the body of a man; the moonlight reflecting off his short blond hair. I can just make out the Bennett Street Rebels tattoo on the right side of his neck. His body sways in the night's gentle breeze, the gale from earlier having relented.

Beside the knot on the railing, is another. The knot is connected to a noose that has not been thrown over the side of the barrier towards the fast-flowing waters of the River Mersey below, though it has still been slipped over the head of a woman. She is wearing a light summer dress and high heels. Her shoulder length hair is wavy and red lipstick accentuates her plump lips. She is standing, hands on the metal railing, looking down at the body. The horror of what she has done fills her eyes.

'Miss Marchand?' I venture, breaking the silence.

She turns slowly, trance like, towards me. The loose noose swivels on her neck, the knot ending up just underneath her chin.

'I'm supposed to kill myself now. That was the agreement. But I can't.'

She sounds calm, despite the scene. She has one foot on the bottom railing, as if caught in two minds, the space between the heel and the sole balancing on the metal like a gymnast. The roar of the Mersey below us and the smell of the water remind me of Summer holidays as a child; the sandy beaches and bustling cafes of busy seaside towns; our usual haunts.

'Who told you that you had to kill yourself?'

'I want to. At least—I did. Now that I'm here…' she shouts, trailing off.

I realise that now is not the time to be worming answers out of her. Instead, I quietly try to convince her that ending her life is not a good idea. She seems uncertain at first. Tears begin to fall down her face, slowly, then in droves, as the realisation of what she has done dawns on her. She slips the noose from around her neck and throws the end over the railings, the loop dangling ominously, though thankfully empty.

Manon collapses onto the steel plate below her feet and I bend down to hug her, to assure her that she is safe. Eventually, I pull her to a standing position and we ascend the stairs.

Police officers are on hand at the top of the bridge to apprehend her. I tell the officers that I'd like some time with her, and that I am more than happy to drive her to the station myself once I'm finished with her. I lead her to my car and put her in the back seat. I call Liam over and tell him to keep an eye on her until I'm finished at the scene.

'Do you want me to try and get some information out of her?' he asks.

'I don't think she's ready,' I reply. He winks at me and slips into the passenger seat. I hear him introduce himself as he closes the door, and the car locks click as I walk away.

By the time I cross the road again, police tape has been rolled across both sides of the bridge, closing the A6 both ways. Tape has also been secured across both sets of steps leading to the metal platform under the bridge. A police officer positioned at the top of each, making sure no one enters. Efficient police work.

As I am about to head down the steps again, I spot a homeless man curled up underneath a set of metal seats across the road in a bus stop. I walk across and when he sees me approaching, he pushes his sleeping bag off and sits up. He reaches out a hand and I shake it, feeling the calluses and dry skin.

'Bit of bother, officer?' he asks.

'There is. Have you been here long?'

'A few hours, I'd say. Though time passes differently in this dimension.'

Hmm. I'm not sure what he's talking about.

'You haven't seen anything out of the ordinary, have you?'

'Afraid not, officer.' As is often the way when it comes to criminal activity, no-one wants to say anything for fear of being called a grass. Snitches get stitches. Snitches end up in ditches, and all that. 'The only thing that I can think of is seeing a pretty sporty car. He roared all the way down the road like a dickhead and then his exhaust did that thing where it sounds like a gunshot. I shit myself. He parked up on the side an hour or so ago. Thought he was dropping somebody off at the pub.'

'Was he with someone?'

'Yeah. He lifted his mate out of the passenger seat. The man was all over the show. The driver had to hold him up.'

'What did he do with him?'

He shrugs his shoulders. 'I didn't take too much notice, to be honest. Just another drunk in Stockport on a Saturday night.'

I thank him for his time and walk back across the road, ducking underneath the police tape. I slip into some overalls and descend the steps down to the platform again.

Since the area is small, Martin has assembled a minimalistic team. Bright spotlights have been set up and some of the team are on their hands and knees, combing the area for anything of note. The police photographer is just finishing snapping the body in situ and Martin begins talk of getting it up onto the platform, ready for John to work his magic.

One of the team holds up a strip of thin, black plastic. An angular cut, probably administered by scissors, stops it from being a complete loop.

'Cable tie,' I say, examining it up close. 'Only one?'

He nods his head. 'So far.'

The thud of feet on steps reverberates under the bridge, before John Kirrane joins us on the platform. Martin orders some of the SOCO team upstairs, to clear room for the body. John leans over the barrier and has a quick look at what he is about to be dealing with. He makes a few notes, runs his finger over the rope holding the body to the bridge and asks for the body to be brought up to the platform. With considerable effort, the team pull on the rope, bringing the deadweight of the body over the railings. Once laid out on the floor, John performs a series of checks, including taking the temperature and finding out whether rigor mortis has set in. Once he is happy that everything has been completed to his high standards, he sets about examining the injuries.

'As I suspected,' he says, feeling both sides of the neck, 'A broken neck. The hyoid bone feels out of place. Of course, I'll need to x-ray the body to confirm it as cause of death.'

'Would the drop cause that, rather than strangulation?' I ask.

'I'd agree with that, taking into consideration the injury and the drop. I believe he fell just over two metres, judging by the length of the rope. Any less, he might not have died straight away. Any more and his head might have come clean off.'

He points to the man's wrists. Thin lines have been cut into the skin, though not deep enough to draw blood.

'Cable ties,' I say. 'One of the SOCOs found one earlier.'

'The other is probably in the river, long gone. But we can do a match with the one that was found.' He points to the tattoo and then to the second noose. 'I'm expecting the other body has floated down the river.'

'We have her,' I tell him, and his eyes light up. 'She killed him and was supposed to kill herself, but couldn't go through with it. She's in the car with Liam. We're taking her back to the station now for questioning.'

'The net closes,' he replies with a smile. 'As always, results of the autopsy will be with you as soon as possible.'

I do one last scan of the scene before leaving to return to the car. Manon is still weeping and Liam looks uncomfortable in the front seat. I give his thigh a little slap as I start the car and begin to drive in the direction of the station. The illuminated clock on the dashboard tells me it's a few minutes before one o'clock. Aside from a car that has just pulled out of a side street behind us, the roads are very quiet.

'Manon,' I say, trying to interrupt the sobbing. 'Can you tell us what happened tonight?'

She continues sobbing, though the time between each heave increases. As she draws breath to speak, the car that has been following us up the deserted A6 suddenly speeds up. The blue-tinged headlights become blinding full beams, and as I flick the mirror to anti-glare setting, the car pulls out onto the overtaking lane. As it draws level with us, three loud bangs fill the air.

Gunshots.

The rear passenger window smashes and Manon screams. I slam the breaks on and pull the car over to the side of the road. The sports car that was following us drifts at high speed with a loud screech into a street opposite and disappears into the darkness. By the time the car has stopped, Liam has already jumped into the back seat and is attempting to stem the blood-flow coming from Manon's shoulder and neck with his jacket. She is writhing in agony.

'Get us to the hospital,' Liam shouts.

I pull the steering wheel and manoeuvre the car onto the other side of the road, moving at speed in the opposite direction, towards Stepping Hill hospital. I can hear Liam trying to keep Manon calm, whispering to her that everything will be OK.

'Did you get a good look at the car?' Liam asks.

'Not a good look,' I reply. 'But enough of one to know that it was Olly Pilkington's.'

18

THE COLD, METAL seat in the hospital's waiting room is making my bottom numb. I stand up and wiggle, trying to get some blood flowing, just as Liam rounds the corner with two steaming cups of coffee.

'Still nothing?' he asks, passing the coffee to me.

'Nothing,' I reply, before taking a huge gulp and burning my tongue.

We sit in silence for a few minutes, intermittently sipping from our cups.

'Are you OK?' he says. When I look over at him, I can see that he looks worried.

'Yeah. Why?'

'It's just… usually, you're so steadfast. You just seem… I don't know… quiet.'

I think about my visit here yesterday, the joyful feeling that I walked out the door with at seeing the little bundle of cells, my little bundle of cells on the screen. The miracle of life. It seems a million years ago now.

'We've just been shot at,' I reply. 'Those bullets could've hit anyone of us. It could be us in there, in the throes between life and death.'

He nods. The enormity of what has just happened is not lost on him.

'I've got a secret,' I say. 'I'm going to tell you, but you're not allowed to tell anyone else, OK?'

Liam looks worried but nods his head.

'Tom and I were here yesterday…'

'Oh my God,' Liam interrupts loudly, clapping his hands to his cheeks. 'What's wrong?'

His drama queen reaction makes me laugh.

'Let me finish. Tom and I were here yesterday to visit the maternity unit. Liam, I'm going to have a baby.'

At first, he looks confused. Then, his face breaks into a wide grin and he jumps out of his seat, pulls me out of mine and locks me to his body with the tightest hug I've ever had.

'That's amazing! Oh, after all the shit you went through after your operation…' He drifts off as tears start. He was just about to release me, but the emotion causes him to pull me even tighter.

'I'm only eleven weeks, so you can't tell anyone, swear?'

He pinkie promises me.

'One last thing,' I add as we take our seats again. 'Tom and I discussed it and we would love it if you'd agree to be the godfather. No pressure if…'

Before I can finish my sentence, I'm in his arms again; his body heaving as he sobs frantically. His reaction is contagious and I can feel my body respond in kind. Before long, it looks like we have just been informed of the death of a close relative.

The door to the waiting room opens and a doctor enters. He has a grim look on his face, though it turns to confusion at the sight of us.

'Everything OK?' he asks.

We manage to regain our composure and assure him that everything is fine, before sitting back down on our seats. He stands over us, and suddenly I feel like a primary school child being talked to by the headteacher.

'She's alive, but we need to get her to theatre. The shoulder wound is superficial, but the neck one is a definite threat to life. We think we can operate successfully, though. She's lucky, if the bullet had entered her neck a few centimetres higher, she would've had no chance.'

'Can we see her?'

He shakes his head.

'She's not in a state to see anyone. We're hoping to operate soon, so I'd give it twenty-four hours or so.'

Having filled him in previously about how she came to be injured, I tell him that I will arrange for a uniformed police officer to keep watch over her, in the unlikely event of the killer coming to finish the job. The doctor agrees that this is a good course of action, shakes our hands and then leaves us alone again.

'You're sure it was Olly's car that you saw?' Liam asks.

'I'm not one hundred percent certain, but it was that orangey-red colour and it had that stupidly wide spoiler.'

'Did it have the personalised number plates?'

'They were covered up.'

'Right,' he says, standing up. 'Let's get over there and see what he has to say?'

'You don't think we should wait for CCTV of the area?'

'No,' he replies, adopting an action movie narrators voice. 'Let's strike while the iron is hot.'

ON THE WAY to Olly Pilkington's house in the east of the city, and in between the questions about my baby from Liam, I consider the car I saw. I'd convinced myself that it was Olly's car on the basis of a spoiler and a colour. The colour could have been cast by the streetlights, and any number of cars could have a spoiler I think is ridiculous, but is quite on trend for the speedy boy racer scene.

In reality, I didn't see the make or model of the car, the number plates or the driver. I'm certain that whoever was driving the car was the person behind tonight's murder as well as the two murder-suicides we're already investigating. There is just no way to be certain that it was Olly Pilkington behind the wheel.

As we pull up outside Olly's house, I notice that his car has been parked at an angle, as if it mounted the kerb at speed and was hastily abandoned. The obnoxious personalised number plates are on full view and a pair of pink, fluffy dice hang from the rear-view mirror. I touch the bonnet, but there is no heat.

Despite that, my certainty that this was the car that followed us and from which the gunshots were fired increases. Even in the little amount of light the middle of the night has to offer, the shimmering in the orange paint job is evident, marking the car as identifiable.

Music blasts out of Olly's house and as we approach, the front door opens and a young woman in towering heels totters out. She pushes past us without looking and makes her way down the front path. When she gets to the gate, she takes a cigarette from her bag and shelters from the wind, in an attempt to light it. She has left the front door open and we give it a perfunctory knock before entering.

Inside the house is a mess. The throbbing beat of the dance music is disorientating and thick plumes of smoke accentuated by the low lighting make it hard to see. We push open the door to the living room where the music is coming from and are greeted by a mass of bodies. Most don't notice us, but a couple prod someone near them and motion to the door. The air is thick with the stench of marijuana, and some people quickly discard a ready-to-be-lit joint. Some grab a handful of their belongings—jackets and handbags—and make haste through the kitchen and out of the back door, knocking over bottles of beer as they go.

When the room has been emptied of his fickler friends, a small group remain. Most are known to the police for gang related trouble. Amongst them is Matty Richards, a man who has been in and out of prison over the years for violent offences. The type of mindless, malleable thug perfect for a gang leader to shape and take advantage of. A small mirror rests on the sofa's arm, thin white powdery lines snaking across it. Matty makes no attempt to hide it. The people in the room fix us with malevolent stares, though no one speaks a word. Liam walks across to the wireless speaker and presses a button, silencing the din.

'Where's Olly?' he says, addressing the room.

'Olly who?' replies Matty, his voice deep and gravelly from too many cigarettes, to the general merriment of the drunken room.

The laughter stops when the door opens and Olly walks in, pulling up his zip with a wide grin on his face and a pretty girl in tow. The smile vanishes when he sees us.

'Oh look! It's gay boy and his ugly little fag hag. What the fuck are you two doing here?' he booms, closing the door behind him and his lady friend.

He swaggers past us and squeezes onto the sofa beside Matty, while the girl walks past us and joins a group on the other side of the room. I get the feeling that Olly sees Matty very much as his henchman and personal security. He grabs a cigarette from a packet on the arm of the sofa and lights it. He takes a deep drag and blows a mouthful of smoke towards the ceiling. The atmosphere feels heavy, as if the assembled are anticipating something big going down.

'I think you know,' Liam says. 'Now, we can do this in private or we can embarrass you in front of your mates. I'm happy with either. Your choice.'

'I've not done anything,' Olly replies calmly.

'That might be the case, but we'd still like a little chat down at the station.'

'He said he hasn't done anything,' Matty says, 'so why would he go to the station with you?'

'Are you his spokesman?' asks Liam, smirking. I flash Liam a look to try and tell him to reign his attitude in. This type of posturing only does one thing to these types of lads—winds them up.

Matty attempts to stand but is pushed down by Olly, who does get up. He takes two steps towards Liam.

'I don't need a fucking spokesperson. I've told you, there is no reason for me to go to the station because I haven't done anything. Can you get that through your thick fucking skull?'

Olly takes another step and pokes his finger into the side of Liam's head. I move towards the two of them as Liam grabs Olly by the wrist and pushes him away. In turn, Olly grabs Liam by the throat with his spare hand and holds him at arm's length. Liam lets go of Olly's wrist and punches the forearm of the limb that is holding his throat. The two men get into close quarters and as the fists begin to fly, I move towards them, though I am knocked to the floor by a solid mass behind me.

I look up to see that it was Matty, rising from the sofa with the speed of a cheetah. His eyes are dilated and white powder frosts the coarse hair on his upper lip. From the floor, I can see a metallic glint in his hand as he lunges at the grappling pair. I manage to grab his leg, but it doesn't slow his momentum.

'No,' screams Olly, his thick Mancunian accent cutting through the noises of the scuffle. The remaining people in the room jump from where they are and leave the house, streaming out the front and back doors.

Matty pulls back from the pair. In his drugged-up state, it seems he can't quite comprehend what he has done. He looks at Liam, then at Olly, and finally at the serrated knife he is holding. Blood coats the blade all the way up to the handle. Mechanically, he wipes it on his trousers, before throwing it to the opposite side of the room where it bounces off the wall. He then throws the living room door back and runs out of the house. I feel detached from everything that has just happened. From the floor, all I can do is watch, like everything that is playing out in front of me is part of a film.

Liam eyes lock onto mine as he stumbles and falls against a shelving unit, knocking some DVDs to the floor. He is clutching his neck, but blood is dripping through his fingers, soaking the sleeve of his shirt and staining the already filthy carpet. Olly hovers over him for a split second, before flashing me an almost apologetic look and following Matty's lead by running out of the house.

WHISPERS IN THE DARK

Being alone with Liam stirs me into action. I pull out my phone and dial 999, screaming the address and describing what has happened. I throw the phone and kneel beside him, pulling his head onto my lap. I grab a blanket from the sofa and press it to the gash in his neck.

From the amount of blood spurting from the wound, I can tell that the knife has probably severed the carotid artery. I repeat over and over for him to stay with me, though I start to panic as his eyes become glassy and unfocussed and his breathing becomes laboured. The blood pools around his head in the shape of a halo. With considerable effort, his cold hand reaches up and takes hold of mine. He mumbles something thorough quivering lips that I can't hear, so I lean closer.

'You're going to be an amazing mummy,' he whispers, shortly before he takes his last breath in my arms.

19

I SIT AT my desk; computer off, coat on, and reflect on the past few hours. I think about the paramedics, entering the house too late to do anything, except confirm there was no pulse. I think of DCI Bob, bursting through the living room door and holding me as I howled and raged. I think about John Kirrane; a man who professionally has seen and tended to probably thousands of dead bodies, mumbling his disbelief as he checked Liam's body and took it away.

And now, as I await someone coming to take my statement, I consider what it must've taken for Bob to walk into that house. Just over a week ago, he was one of the first on scene at the murder of one of his oldest friends. A few days later, he learnt that not only was his friend dead, but that in his last few minutes, he'd taken someone else's life as well as his own. Now, here he was, consoling me, as he learned of the death of someone he considered a son.

I rest my head on my desk and the tears flow freely as I consider the fact that Liam's death was entirely my fault. We went to Olly's house on the understanding that I had identified his car as the one who shot at ours. But I'd doubted that, hadn't I? I should've made it clearer that I wasn't sure and certain. I should've drummed home to him that I don't know a fucking thing about cars. And now he's gone. He's gone. I hammer my fists on the desk until my knuckles begin to bleed. I need a release from the pain coursing through my veins.

The tears continue to fall as Dylan, his husband, swims into my mind. The broad smile on his wedding day that I'd envied, the happiness etched on his face for the world to see forevermore. The way they held each other close, grasping at each other as if millimetres between them would somehow spell disaster. The intimacy they had displayed in such a public space, the bravery that took. And suddenly, a rugby ball tumbles into my mind's eye, bouncing awkwardly in the way an egg-shaped ball does. I think of the honeymoon—the Rugby World Cup in Japan and all the other future plans Liam and Dylan had together. How adoption might've been something they envisaged. How the pitter patter of tiny feet could've completed their little family. And now, all of those designs for life had disappeared. All at the hands of a coke-fuelled thug.

There's a knock at the door. My head snaps up and I silently thank whoever is outside that they are not one of those people who knocks and then bursts in, whether invited or not. I wipe my eyes, though I know that there is nothing I can do for the blotchy redness on my cheeks, nor the bulging vein in my forehead.

I tell whoever is outside to come in and a uniformed police officer enters, looking a little guilty. I know how he must be feeling. The death of a police officer, from bottom rank to top, is felt by everyone in the job, even if you didn't know them. There's the knowledge that it could've been you. You want justice. You want to know that whoever has caused this pain is going to get his just desserts. Sadly, getting that justice sometimes means doing things at a time that doesn't seem appropriate. Like interviewing the dead detective's partner.

'Sorry about the timing,' he says sheepishly, slipping into the seat opposite me.

I give my statement, detailing the events of the night. Being so versed in collecting them, I try to give the pertinent details and exclude any extraneous facts. The bare bones are that Matty Richards stabbed Detective Sergeant Liam Sutton to death with a kitchen knife in an unprovoked attack.

He thanks me for my time, utters his condolences and leaves the room, notepad in hand. I push myself out of my chair, collect my belongings from under the table and make my way out the door. Though the main room houses over a dozen tables and is currently full, the atmosphere is subdued, the loss felt by everyone. I cross the room, making no effort to engage with anyone, thankful that I'm left alone. I press the button on the lift and listen to the mechanical hum from inside the shaft. When the door opens, I'm startled by DCI Bob squeezing through the doors before they are fully open.

'Ah, Erika,' he says, looking up from the piece of paper in his hand. 'Can I see you in my office?'

I follow him back across the room and into his office, the frosted glass front appearing inviting whilst offering an air of privacy. He walks around the heavy oak desk and eases himself into his comfortable swivel chair, sighing as he takes a load off. I move the less comfortable chair from the side of the room so that it is facing him, and then fall into it, exhausted.

'Kiddo,' he says, 'I'm so sorry you have had to go through this tonight. Liam was a great man and a hell of a detective.'

We share a silence.

'Did he tell you about the promotion?' he asks.

I shake my head.

'He was about to be promoted to Detective Inspector. I'd let him know a few days ago. I thought he might have shared it.'

The news of Liam's promotion forces tears I didn't know were left down my face. I think of the crimes he could've prevented and the cases he could've solved, and I think about the enormous loss I, and the police, have just suffered. The fact he hadn't told me sums up the man; the case came first, personal glories irrelevant. Even when I'd shared my baby news with him, he'd kept shtum, allowing me my time in the spotlight.

'As such,' he continues, 'we'd already appointed a new DS in his place. His name is Andy Robinson. He's transferring here from Liverpool. He was supposed to be starting in a few weeks' time, but in light of what has happened, he'll probably be here at the start of the week.'

'Jesus,' I say, my voice loud, 'Liam's barely taken his last fucking breath and you've already fucking replaced him.'

'Liam can never be replaced,' he counters, kindly keeping his voice calm. 'Like I said, it was already arranged and I have a case to think about.'

I can't imagine the pressure Bob is under, but I still feel like a petulant teenager as I stare sullenly at a nondescript spot on the floor.

'We'll talk about it further at a better time,' he says.

Just then, a shadowy figure knocks on the door and opens it, revealing herself as Angela.

'Boss,' she says, looking at me. 'Someone is here, asking to see you.'

I rise from my seat without another word to Bob, turn and walk out the door, following Angela to the reception desk. A small gasp escapes me when I see who is standing there, waiting for me. He is casually leaning against the wall, knee bent with one foot on the surface behind him. His casual body language is cancelled out by the apprehensive look on his face and the large red welt on the side of his head.

Olly Pilkington.

I feel like a shard of ice has pierced my heart. I can feel the adrenaline flood my veins and my first instinct is to run around the desk and kick the shit out of him.

'What the fuck are you doing here?' I ask, surprised at the uncontrollable rage in my voice.

He looks at me, his eyes wide, perhaps shocked at a helpful member of the police using that kind of language.

'I just want to clear my name.'

I take a step towards him, but Angela moves between us. The blood is thumping in my ears and her words sound distorted as she tells him to follow her to one of the interview rooms. The most feared gang boss in the city walks past me with an easy confidence, and it takes everything in me not to swing for him. Instead, I sink into the receptionist's chair and close my eyes.

I imagine Liam, ice running through his veins, urging me to keep my cool. To think of the bodies; of the families of the dead who need justice, of the case that needs solving. I get out of the squeaky chair and follow Angela and Olly to the interview room. DCI Bob intercepts me on the way.

'Why has Olly Pilkington turned up?' he asks.

'He wants to clear his name, apparently.'

He looks unconvinced.

'I'll take this,' he says. 'You sit this one out.'

I shake my head.

OLLY SITS ON the opposite side of the table to Bob and me. Some of the confidence on show only half an hour ago has been lost. We sat him in the room for about twenty minutes, alone, and watched as he became a little nervous, judging by his body language; the jiggling leg, the beads of sweat. I'm sure he's been interviewed many times, but never in connection with a dead police officer. He must know how much trouble he is in to even be here. Olly Pilkington is many things, but stupid he is not.

I start the recording and state who is present, the date and time. As I'm talking, I realise how hoarse my voice is; the long day and night, coupled with all the crying, has really taken its toll. Bob seems to notice, as he speaks first and takes the lead.

'Now, Mr Pilkington, I think you realise how much trouble you could be in, so I want you to shoot straight with me.'

Olly gulps audibly, his protruding Adam's Apple bobbing up and down. He fiddles with the sleeve of his striped shirt, pulling it down over his forearm and buttoning the cuff around his wrist.

'Where were you tonight?' begins Bob.

'At my house.'

'All night?'

'Yes. We were having a party. As you know,' he adds, looking at me, though I don't meet his eyes.

'Was the party in aid of anything?'

'It's my birthday.'

He looks at us like he expects us to wish him many happy returns. Instead, Bob pulls out a manila folder and leafs through it before pulling out a collection of photographs and spreading them over the table. The eyes of Marcus, Clive, Kai, Zoe, Manon and the as-yet unidentified hanging man stare up at us.

'Do you know any of these people?'

'I've seen these two before,' he says, pointing to Marcus and Kai. 'They're members—'

'Of the rival gang to yours,' interrupts Bob.

Olly nods.

'So you have reason to want them dead.'

'I have never, and will never, kill anyone. Look,' he says, his eyes dropping. 'I've done some stupid shit in my time, but I'd never take a life.'

'Except one of my detectives.'

'I didn't kill him,' he says, glancing up at me. 'Tell him.'

'Who did?' Bob asks, though he already knows the answer.

'Matty Richards. The guy has been a liability for years. When I tried to convince him to come with me, he did this,' he says, pointing at the vicious swelling on the right side of his face.

It can't be five hours since the stabbing happened. I realise then that Olly Pilkington is nothing but a coward. Here he is, trying to save his own skin, by ratting out his mate. He's taken a punch for his troubles, trying to coerce his friend—the killer—to come to the station with him, and wants to be treated like some sort of war hero. It takes all the restraint in my body not to jump across the table and add to the cuts and bruises already on show.

Angela knocks on the door, opens it and hands me a piece of paper. It is a black-and-white photo, taken from a CCTV camera. It shows my car being pursued by the sports car, probably ten seconds before he pulled level with us and opened fire. I thank Angela and she leaves. I push the photos of the deceased to one side of the table and set the CCTV photo in front of Olly.

'Is this your car?' I ask baldly.

He shakes his head and reaches into his pocket, retrieving his phone. He sets it flat on the table so that we can see what he is up to. He accesses his photos and scrolls up until he comes to a series of images of an orange car with tinted windows and a wide spoiler. He spins the phone around so that I can see it more clearly.

'I drive a Nissan Skyline,' he says, pointing to the badge of the car on the phone screen. He lifts the CCTV picture and studies it. 'This is a Mitsubishi Evo. It's got a similar spoiler but mine has racing stripes and this doesn't.'

I get up from my seat and leave the room, walking as quickly as I can to the toilet. I crash into a cubicle and vomit into the toilet bowl. I killed Liam. If I hadn't been so hasty to identify the car as Olly's, we would never have gone over there. It was sloppy police work, and sloppy police work gets people killed. *My* sloppy police work got Liam killed.

I go to the sink and wash away the gunk from my chin. When I leave the toilets, I walk to my office. I walk over to the evidence board, and pin up pictures of Manon and the hanging man, as well as the CCTV picture of the car chasing us. I pull off the picture of Olly Pilkington and look at what we're left with.

Five dead.

One fearful French suicidal killer who I doubt had anything to do with any of the other murders.

No suspects.

One dead detective sergeant. Scratch that. One dead friend.

Fuck.

20

I WAKE UP. The sunlight is streaming through the curtains, causing my face to wrinkle. For a few glorious seconds, reality doesn't register and I simply lie in my bed, under the covers, peaceful. Then, the realisation of why I am lying in my bed, fully clothed, at just after three o'clock in the afternoon, comes crashing down like a foaming wave on a fragile shale beach. All the little pieces of me; the trillions of atoms that make up my body, rattle together, causing my vision to blur, my ears to buzz and my stomach to contract.

I pick up my phone and access the photos, scrolling up to the images of Liam's wedding, a few short weeks ago. I study each picture intently; Liam and Dylan walking up the aisle hand in hand, beaming at each other, about to be married. Liam, behind a long table filled with ornate glasses of champagne, microphone pressed to his lips making his speech, everyone else in the photo smiling at whatever it was he was saying. Liam on the dancefloor; mellow lighting, grinning at the crowd as he holds Dylan tight during their first dance. The twinkle in his eyes causes me to simultaneously cry out loud and beam with pride.

I throw the phone down on the bed and reach for the water on my bedside table and gulp half of the contents of the glass down. I replace it and reach for the post-traumatic stress tablets that the doctor prescribed. Instead, my fingers slip over a thin piece of paper that I can't remember putting there. I grasp it and a little gasp escapes my lips.

In the midst of all the sadness, I'd almost forgotten about my baby. Though the photo of the scan is fuzzy, I can still make out an arm and two legs. A little arm that, right now, in my womb, might be scratching his forming nose or touching the umbilical cord which is pumping life into him. I realise that I'm already thinking of the baby as a boy, through nothing but pure guesswork.

My mum used to say 'one in, one out' when considering life and death, and I used to think they were empty words. She said it stoically when the tumour was found in her brain a few weeks after finding out about my sister's pregnancy and repeated it three weeks later on her death bed. I'm sure she'd say it now about Liam and my little bundle of cells. One in, one out. And I realise that they are not empty words, that in fact they are full of compassion and love.

I resolve to do everything I can to give the baby the best start. Grabbing the tablet packages from the top of the bedside table, I march to the bathroom and pop the remaining tablets out of the foil packaging and into the toilet. Once they have all been popped, I flush the chain and watch as they swirl away from me. Instantly, I feel like a weight has been lifted, like I am no longer a slave to the medication.

I walk downstairs and greet Tom with a kiss. I sit on the sofa beside him and tell him all about Liam. He'd heard. DI Bob had taken the liberty of calling him. Tom says that since I'd looked so peaceful in the night, he couldn't bear to wake me. Instead, he'd sat with a glass of whiskey downstairs and finally crawled into bed around ten this morning, but couldn't get to sleep. This is the first time we share our grief. Tom and Liam were good friends, having worked many cases together when Tom was part of the police service.

We sit for a long time, swapping and sharing stories about him, and by the end of it, my cheeks are sore from smiling. I check my phone and realise that I have a missed call and a voicemail from the hospital. The audio message tells me that Manon's operation was a success, and that she is ready for a short visit.

'Isn't it a bit soon to be thinking about the case?' Tom asks when I tell him my plans for the afternoon. 'Bob told me that he told you to take as much time off as you need.'

I know Tom is just trying to protect me, but he knows as well as anyone that in a case, time is an enemy. I assure him that I will be fine and that I will see him later. I run up the stairs, spray some deodorant and make myself look half decent. Tom strokes my stomach as I walk past him and out of the house.

THE HOSPITAL CAR park is full, and it takes a few laps around it before I spot someone pulling out. Once the space is free, I pull in and make my way to the pay station. When we were here for the maternity unit visit the other day, Tom had paid and hadn't shared that he'd needed to re-mortgage the house to stay for an hour. I stare in disbelief at the extortionate amount it takes to park here, before emptying the contents of my purse into the machine and taking the ticket.

The lack of windows and low-level lighting casts a green hue over the hospital reception, making everyone look ill, whether they are or not. Most of the seats in the waiting room are taken up. Some people are reading magazines while they wait for their appointments, some chew at nails or stare into space, lost in their own little worlds of worry. My shoes slap on the tiled floor, causing some of those waiting to look up with disapproval in their eyes.

The reception desk is being manned by a pencil thin, saggy-eyed woman. She smiles at the man who is talking to her, though his body language looks a tad aggressive. When he turns away suddenly and I get a good look at his face, I recognise him. He marches off towards the door and I follow him, holding my finger up at the confused receptionist.

'Richard,' I say to the vicar's back.

He stops close to the doors, which slide open due to his proximity, allowing a welcome rush of cool air to enter. His forehead wrinkles and I can tell he is struggling to place me.

'DI Erika Piper,' I say, and I notice the lines on his forehead smooth out as recognition dawns.

'How are you, detective?'

'Fine,' I say, not wishing to go into the details of my last twenty-four hours. 'Are you ok?'

'Yes,' he nods. 'I'm supposed to be seeing a member of the congregation who sadly isn't too well, though they won't let me in. The woman at reception says that Linda's daughter specified family only. I tried to explain that I'd promised her, that Linda herself had asked me to visit, but she's having none of it. I left a note for her, so hopefully she'll know I haven't just forgotten about her.'

'Bureaucracy, eh?' I smile. 'Does the name Charlie Hill mean anything to you?'

I'd had a message from John Kirrane on the way to the hospital confirming the hanging body as Charlie Hill, formerly of Bennett Street.

Richard considers the name for a moment before shaking his head. 'I don't think so, why?'

'He was a member of the Bennett Street Rebels. He was found dead last night. I was wondering if he had ever popped by the church.'

'Another body? Goodness me, what is the world coming to?' He looks thoroughly saddened by the news. 'It's entirely possible that he did come to an outreach session, though I don't recognise the name. However, some of the lads gave fake names. Some only ever saw me and some only saw Jack.'

'Why?'

'Timing. Preference. I'm not sure really,' he says. 'We tried to help in any way we could, and if that meant they were more comfortable discussing things with one of us, that's what we did.'

'If we were to bring a picture of Charlie to you, could you confirm if he was one of the lads you saw?'

'Absolutely,' he replies. 'Anything I can do to help you get to the bottom of this evil.'

I thank him for his time and make a mental note to talk to Jack, having heard a lot about him but not actually having met him yet.

Richard shakes my hand and leaves. I walk back to the unoccupied, but busy, receptionist. She sets a clipboard to one side, blows a stray blonde hair out of her eye and smiles sweetly at me. I introduce myself and disclose the reason for my visit, flashing my police identification over the top of the desk. She gives me easy to follow directions, which take me straight to Manon's room.

A police officer sits in an uncomfortable chair outside her room and looks positively delighted when I relieve him of duty, albeit temporarily. He walks down the corridor, stretching as many muscles as he can with some impromptu yoga-esque moves. I knock softly on the door and enter.

Manon lies on her bed, propped up by a number of thin pillows with an IV bag suspended above her head. A clear plastic tube snakes into the crook of her left arm. Her hair has been tied up, exposing the stitched wound on her neck. She averts her attention from the tennis match on the small television and smiles groggily at me as I sit in the chair beside her.

The first thing she does is thank me for saving her life. For a while we discuss the operation and her stay in hospital so far. She seems reasonably pain free, given her injuries, though that could be down to the medication. The atmosphere changes slightly when I take out a notepad and assume a more authoritative role. Her body becomes more rigid, and the smile disappears.

'Are you still feeling suicidal?'

She shakes her head.

'What made you want to commit suicide in the first place?'

The questions may seem a tad cold, but I need answers as quickly as I can get them. I can see her lip quivering, but I let the silence unfold between us. Eventually, she speaks, her voice quivering.

'I moved to the UK with my boyfriend. We both wanted to learn English better, so I became an au pair. I found out that he was cheating on me, not long ago. When I confronted him, he broke up with me. My parents told me it was a bad idea, moving to a new country with a boy, but I thought I knew best. I had no friends to talk to about it, very little money, and I couldn't call my parents because they'd made it clear that if I went, I couldn't come home.'

'They said that?' I ask, incredulously.

'Well, it was implied.'

'Can you tell me about last night?'

She looks scared and I assure her that the worst is over. That she might be able to give us information to make all this stop.

'Well, I arrived at the bridge and when I went down the steps and under the platform, there was the body waiting for me like I'd been told. He was on the outside of the railings…'

'Balancing?' I ask.

'No,' she replies, shaking her head. 'He was held to the railings by his wrists. They had some sort of material around it. His neck was already through the noose and when I cut them, he dropped immediately. I thought he was going to fall in the river, but then I heard the crack.'

Of his neck. Those three words remain unspoken.

'Then I threw the scissors over the railing like I'd been told. I slipped the noose over my neck and then I freaked out. I imagined touching the other body on the way down. Or the rope breaking and being washed away by the water. I couldn't do it. That's when I called you.'

'You keep saying you were told to do this? Who made you?'

'The Guide,' she replies.

'And how did he tell you what to do?'

'When I decided I wanted to die…' she trails off, tears beginning to flow down her face. She composes herself, replacing the glasses on her nose. 'When I decided I wanted to die, I went on the internet to find a sure-fire way to do it. I didn't want to mess it up and paralyse myself or something. I found a website that you could use to talk to others. Discuss ideas. That kind of thing. Then, one day I woke up and I had an invite into the member's area from an account called The Guide. I accepted, and he told me that he would make killing myself easy. Then, he suggested that, since I was going to die, that I could also kill a baddie.'

'A baddie?' I repeat. The urge to laugh at such baby-ish language in the midst of all this violence and death is almost overwhelming. I just about manage to turn a small snigger into a series of unconvincing coughs.

'That's not what he called them, but it's what he meant. He told me this person had done nasty things and deserved to die, and that he would make it easy for me. He told me everything would be ready, and all I'd have to do is follow his instructions. He told me that if I agreed, he'd make killing myself an easy thing to do. He'd arrange everything and clear up afterwards so that I wouldn't get in trouble. So that it looked like I'd been killed. I said yes. I don't know why.'

'What is the name of the website?'

She lets out a long sigh.

'My Time to Die.'

21

'AH, ERIKA,' SAYS DCI Bob as I walk through the door of his office. 'Take a seat.'

I follow his orders, striding to the front of the room and sitting in one of the chairs in front of his desk. The other is occupied by a man I have never met before. His dark hair is short and gelled to the side. His stubble is patchy, growing longer in little clumps near each ear. Intense brown eyes are juxtaposed by a wide smile. Good cop and bad cop on the same face. A creased, loose-fitting shirt with an open top button and a poorly knotted tie gives the impression that he got dressed for today last night and slept in these clothes, to save a few minutes this morning.

'Erika, this is Andrew Robinson.'

'Pleased to meet you,' he says, extending his hand. The accent is a mish-mash of Scouse and Scottish. 'You're my partner then, eh?'

I glance at Bob, uncertainty plastered across my face. When Bob had told me about Andrew coming in early, it was never as a direct replacement for Liam. I mean, I knew he was coming as Detective Sergeant, but I didn't know he was going to be my partner. It feels too soon to be given a new partner. I thought I was simply taking him under my wing for a while, to show him the ropes and to settle him into a new job in a new city. A strange feeling rises in my stomach; a mixture of betrayal and something I can't put my finger on. I feel annoyed that Bob has seen fit to replace Liam straight away. I feel even more annoyed that Bob didn't tell me he was going to be my partner, buttering me up instead, by asking if I'd look after him like he is some stray dog.

I can tell I'm being a little dramatic, but with the events of the past forty-eight hours, the lack of sleep and the pregnancy hormones, I feel I'm entitled to be.

'Erika,' I reply. 'Nice to meet you. Do you prefer to be called Andrew or Andy?'

'They called me Robbo back in Liverpool,' he says with a smile.

'I'm not going to call you that,' I say. 'It makes you sound like a footballer, or one of the lads.'

I know I'm being unfriendly, and when his smile falters and he looks awkwardly at Bob, I feel like a bitch. I think of Liam, who always had a smile, even for his worst enemy, and know I should be more like him, but I can't snap out of the mood I am in.

'Andy is fine,' he says.

There's an apology on the tip of my tongue, but my lips remain steadfast in front of it. Instead, I give a curt nod.

'Andy has moved to Marple, maybe you could show him around?' says Bob, trying desperately to lighten the mood.

I nod again. Both men exchange another glance that makes me long for one of my tablets.

'Shall we go to briefing?' asks Andy. 'I'm buzzing to get started.'

'Andy, would you mind giving Erika and I a few minutes alone?' says Bob. 'You know where the briefing room is. Why don't you head there, grab yourself a brew and we'll be with you in a minute or two?'

Andy flashes us both a smile, gets up and leaves the room wordlessly. He hesitates just outside the door, glancing left and right, getting his bearings, before heading unsurely in the right direction.

'What the fuck was that?' asks Bob, his face flushed.

'I'm sorry,' I hear myself saying, like a naughty schoolchild to the headmaster. 'I just didn't know he was replacing Liam as my partner and it threw me.'

'As I've said before, the case comes first. Andy's got an impressive track record, comes highly recommended and seems like a nice lad. Liam, the person, can't be replaced. Liam, the partner, can be and has to be. I know it's not nice to hear, but it's the truth.'

I nod. I know that I can't work alone. I know that I have to have a partner, it's how the job works. And I know that I have been unfair and vow silently to make it right.

'Are you sure you're ok to be here? I did tell you to take as much time as you need.'

'Yeah,' I reply. 'Once the case is over, I might take some time, but right now, I just want to catch the fucker responsible for all this mess.'

I can see the understanding blaze in his eyes.

'One more thing before we go,' he says, his voice softening. 'No-one else really knows this yet, so keep it quiet, but after this case, I'm retiring. The whole thing with Clive, and now Liam, it's too much. I've not really slept since the start of the case, and then seeing Liam's body—he was the same age as my daughter—it's really got to me. I told top brass I'd see this one out and then I'm done.'

He hands me a tissue when he sees that I am crying. Bob has been a father figure to me, especially during the last two years; firstly, with the aftermath of the near fatal stabbing and then, a few weeks later, with the death of my mother. I can't imagine what it's going to be like without him. He's been my boss since I started here.

'I'm pregnant,' I blurt out.

The sadness on his face is replaced immediately. His eyes spring open and he glances down at my stomach.

'But I thought...' he says.

'I know. Miracle baby,' I reply, as he lurches out of his seat and wraps me in his arms.

'I'm so pleased for you,' he says, tears in his own eyes. He straightens up and gives a small laugh as he dabs at his eyes with a tissue. 'What a pair we are, eh?'

'OKAY,' I SAY to the assembled crowd in the briefing room, I now feel calm and collected after the emotional meeting, ready to update the team on what we have, or don't have, to be more precise.

I point to the board containing the evidence so far. On one side of it, six faces stare out at the crowd. Pictures of the five dead and one living. A map of Greater Manchester covers the middle of the board. The smaller map that had been stuck up at the last briefing had to be replaced, due to the third murder/suicide bid's location being further out.

Red pins show the locations of the murders. Since the map shows such a large area, the pins showing the murders at Bennett Street and the church are pretty much on top of each other. The most recent, in Stockport, is about thirty centimetres away. On the far side of the board is Olly Pilkington's face. Since tearing it off, after his appearance at the station, I'd had a change of heart. Just because he flashed his puppy dog eyes and supposedly laid his cards on the table, doesn't take away the years of misery he has caused. Also, I couldn't bear to look at an empty suspect board. The final picture on the board is of the sports car chasing my own.

Every time I look at it, my heart flutters. I remember the gunshots and the danger, the threat to life, but that's not why my body reacts in that way. The reason is because I think of Liam, beside me in the passenger seat. Then, his calmness as he tended to Manon's injuries. The humanity he showed. The quiet voice he used when trying to soothe her. And his own horrible end a few short hours later.

I take the team through what has happened in the case so far, laying the facts out, mainly for Andy's benefit. I tell him about pursuing the Greg lead, and then Olly. He keeps nodding at me, and I can tell he's waiting until I finish to say something. When I do, he does.

'Coming into this with fresh eyes,' he says, 'it looks like Bennett Street is the hotspot. Two murders a stone's throw away from each other is rough.'

'What about the Stockport one then?' I ask.

'I think the killer, or whoever is behind the killings anyway, knows his way around Bennett Street. The first two were him practicing, making sure he could get it right on home turf. Now that he knows he's onto a winning formula, he's expanding his killing zone.'

It's a well-considered, yet chilling, argument.

'Here's the plan,' I say. 'We're going to monitor internet usage in the Bennett Street area. We know whoever is organising this is using a page on the dark web. It's unlikely such a calculating and organised killer will make a careless mistake, but you never know. Angela, can you sort that?'

She scrawls something down in her notepad and gives me a thumbs up.

'Since all three of the murder victims were members of the Bennett Street Rebels, I think it's now safe to assume that they are his targets. We need officers knocking on doors on Bennett Street, warning people not to meet with anyone they don't know.'

'Why would they meet with someone they don't know?' Andy asks.

'Drug meets,' I reply. 'Finally, Manon told me the website she was using, the one she was convinced to become a killer on. I'm going to set up a fake profile and try and get in contact with The Guide. We find The Guide, we find the killer.'

The meeting disbands and people shuffle out of the room. Andy and I are the only ones left and as he moves towards the door, I stop him.

'Andy, I'm sorry for being a dick before…'

He stops me with a wave of his hand.

'Don't worry about it. Bob told me what you've been through in the past few days. It can't be easy. I'm surprised you're even functioning,' he says with a kind smile.

'I barely am.'

'It seems like you're on it. Now, let's catch this killer. Then, we can talk about you calling me Robbo,' he says, and I can't help but laugh.

I SIT ON the sofa and balance the laptop on my knee. I log onto the dark web, once again using the Tor browser installed by Ross, and navigate my way to the My Time To Die site. I'm greeted almost immediately by a roadblock. Or, at least, a temporary set of traffic lights, set to red. The homepage of the site is black. A purple outlined box sits in the middle of the page, the same purple outlines a scythe in the top right-hand corner. The same coloured letters spell out the website's name in block capital within the box. Below them is my stumbling block.

Access to the website is by invite only. There is space for me to fill in my name, location, date of birth and reason for wanting to access the website. Obviously, I'm not going to submit my own details, so I type a fake name and date of birth into the empty boxes and give my reasons for wanting to become a part of the website. When I'm done, Joseph from Stockport—born on April Fool's Day, 1990—wants to become a member so that he can find an efficient way to kill himself. I click submit. When I do, the box disappears and is replaced with a message, telling me that my reasons will be considered and to check back soon to find out if my membership has been successful.

I leave the browser open, set the computer down, and walk to the kitchen. I fill the kettle and flick the switch. I get a cup and shout to Tom, who is on the other sofa in the living room, asking if he wants a coffee too. He replies and I take another cup from the cupboard, covering the bottom with coffee granules. When the kettle has done its job, I fill the cups and add a splash of milk to mine, before returning to the living room. I give Tom his and set mine on the side, waiting for it to cool down. I glance at my laptop to see that the screen has changed.

A purple rectangle, with features added that I assume are trying to make it look like a door, is taking up the centre of the screen. A word, written in the same capital letters and font as the site's name on the previous page, are emblazoned across it. I click on the word ENTER, and the page changes. I was anticipating something dramatic happening—the door swinging open or the Grim Reaper's welcoming finger summoning me in—but the page changes in the same boring way as on the normal web.

I'm taken to a list of rules. I skim read.

I've been given a unique username and password that I'm not allowed to share under any circumstances. My membership with the site will last for one month and then will expire, with no option to extend it. I'm not allowed to tell anyone about the site. I am allowed to discuss death and suicide on the forums, but I'm not allowed to insult anyone or leave judgemental remarks. It states very clearly that this is a place for support and brotherhood, for sharing ideas. If any of these rules are broken, my membership will be terminated immediately. It also explicitly forbids any attempt to meet with other members. If we do, membership will be terminated. We must not print anything off or leave a paper trail. Whoever runs the domain is keen for it to remain solely on screens. A virtual world of death.

I click on the box to confirm that I have read the terms and conditions and a little tick appears. The page once again changes and I am presented with my username—079—and a password, a series of capitalised and non-capitalised letters, mixed with a few numbers. I jot them down into my notebook. I assume that the username, 079, refers to the fact that I am the seventy-ninth person to gain membership to the site.

I navigate to my emails and send a message to forces around the country, explaining how this site has come up in our case and asking if anyone else had encountered it. Surely, if someone has gone to the trouble of setting up a site such as this, it must be national or even international. Someone else in the police must've come across it, or at least have suspicious murder-suicides which may fit our profiles.

I enter the site and take in its very basic layout. There is only one tab at the top, labelled forums. I click on it and am presented with a selection of links which lead to forums which are all self-contained inside the site.

I spend some time searching through the various message threads. In *Depression*, 065 describes the demons in his head that visit daily, screaming at him to end it all. A number of people have replied. Some suggest holding on for a few more days. Give the voice time to go away, and if it doesn't, if it decides to stay, maybe it would be best to follow its advice. Some suggest listening to the voice straight away. Simply take too many of the pills he mentioned he had been prescribed and float off on a cloud of pain relief towards death.

In *Methods,* my predecessor as newest member, 078, states that they are ready to die after the break-up of a marriage. The children blame her and want to live with their father, and that the pain is too much to bear. Several people have replied, suggesting possible methods. It's discussed casually, as if suggesting a baking recipe. The numbers replying to her are either in the late sixties or seventies. I assume that the lower numbers have either used their month's membership or are now dead. I wonder what numbers our killers were.

Tom mutters under his breath and jumps up suddenly, cheering that a football team in blue has just scored a goal. The excitement turns to annoyance as some extra referee in a different part of the country decides that the player who scored the goal was marginally offside. Tom moans about the decision and I think of the triviality of his concerns. Here, on my screen, are people genuinely at their lowest ebb, begging strangers for encouragement to end their lives.

I leave 078's thread and click on the 'post comment' button. A new thread emerges with my number at the top. I type my short message into the dialogue box, check the content, and hit publish. On the screen, my new thread appears at the top of the *Methods* section.

My name is Joseph and I want to die.

22

WHEN I WAKE up, I lift the laptop from beside my bed and log on to My Time To Die, accessing my thread. I have a number of replies, mostly from numbers in the seventies, welcoming me to the site and asking why I want to take my own life. Instead of answering them straight away, I go back to the main thread and peruse my options.

Manon had mentioned that someone called The Guide, presumably whoever was in charge of the website and behind the suicide-murders, had been the one to get in touch with her and to offer her private membership. From navigating the threads I had so far, I'd seen no sign of The Guide interacting with anyone, though I had only been a member for less than twelve hours. My intention to trawl the website last night had been curtailed by a headache, which thankfully now has cleared.

I search through each thread, reading replies and jotting down anything I think will be useful—the name of a town or landmark, a date or a stray surname that someone has mentioned and has forgotten is one of the forbidden rules. Most of the posts are just sad and depressed people shouting into an echo chamber. They're hurting and they want someone to tell them that everything is going to be OK. What they really need, I think, is to visit the Samaritans for a willing ear and helpful advice. In my opinion, they're not a genuine danger to anyone, let alone themselves.

My first sighting of The Guide is on a post where it's obvious that 057 is a danger to themselves and to others. The post is full of vitriol. It's misspelled, as if typed in a flurry of anger. 057 wants to kill himself because he has been wrongfully dismissed from work, in his eyes, at least. Insults and revenge are aimed at his boss. He says he's going to break into his former workplace and kill himself, so that everyone knows it's their fault. But before he does that, his boss is going to suffer. The Guide had commented on the thread, simply stating that he could help with the pain and asking if he'd like to talk privately. 057 had replied with one word—yes—and the conversation, presumably, continued in a heavily encrypted private chat between the two.

Scrolling through the rest of the messages, it seems The Guide had been very selective. During my research of the multiple threads and sub-threads, The Guide had only got in touch with seven members. He only replied to those who showed that they were a danger to others as well as themselves, leaving the needy and the attention seekers alone. Each of the seven were invited to a private chat, and all seven reacted positively to the offer, though whether any became the killers we've found is unclear.

I decide that I need to be more aggressive on my post, so I navigate back to it and click on the replies. 071 and 073 want to know why I, or rather Joseph, want to die. 074 has simply sent me a link of suicide methods and their percentage likelihood of success.

I reply to 071 and copy and paste the same message to 073. I tell them that I just found out my fiancée had been cheating on me, and that I plan on enacting violent revenge on her before killing myself. I make a few spelling mistakes to make it seem like I'm on the edge, unable to control my shaking fingers because of the rage I'm experiencing.

I then log out of the dark web, close the laptop, kiss a sleeping Tom on the forehead before heading to the shower.

ANDY AND I pull up parallel to the church. He hits the kerb and we jerk backwards, almost hitting the car behind us. Andy pulls his mouth to the side, a humorous mix of apology and awkwardness. We get out of the car. Behind us is the steady hum of traffic travelling along the main road. In front of us, the terraced houses of Bennett Street stretch into the distance. Well maintained trees are dotted at regular intervals along the pavement, their lush green leaves lending the street an uplifting feeling. Life amongst the death that the area has encountered recently.

The avenue itself is almost empty, though the road is narrowed by cars on both sides, squeezed close together like sardines. Safety in numbers. There is very little footfall. A solitary, elderly man shuffles towards us, dressed in a green suit he's probably owned for decades, despite the heat. He nods a wordless hello as he passes, a solemn look etched upon his face.

Andy and I begin our plan of action—a good ol' fashioned door-to-door session. Someone along this road must know something. The worrying thing is that one of the people on the other side of these doors could be the next victim. Perhaps, with this knowledge, the residents will be more loose-tongued than normal. Though, seeing as most of them are part of a gang with a deep mistrust of the police, it's a theory which is more fanciful than realistic.

The plan is that Andy takes the even numbered houses on the left and I take the odd numbered houses opposite. We move at roughly the same time, in case one of us needs the other.

After a few houses, it is easy to see that the recent murders have not changed the residents' attitude to the police one iota. Most close the door by the time I have introduced myself. Some, even quicker. A man in one of the houses pulled the curtains open, made eye contact, closed the curtains and did not come to the door. It's frustrating, but we can't force them to talk to us. Yet.

Gazing across the street, I can see Andy is getting the same treatment. As he has an obscenity hurled at him and a door slammed in his face, he turns and marches to the gate. He catches my eye and smiles.

'This is fun,' he shouts across the street.

I smile back at him and give him the thumbs up. He returns it before opening the next gate.

I've been reflecting on my perception of Andy. He is a nice guy, and I was definitely in the wrong in being an ass to him. During the drive over here, I put in extra effort to be nice to him; to get to know him. I asked the questions and listened intently to the answers. Unfortunately, my attention and goodwill was interrupted by the opening guitar riff of *Does Your Mother Know?* The upbeat ABBA hit was one of Liam's favourites and we'd spent many a journey belting it out. All these little reminders keep whispering to me that nothing will ever be the same again. After that, my mood dipped, and I'd retreated into silence. To his credit, Andy was good at reading the situation and simply concentrated on getting us here.

I turn back to my next house and knock on the door. It opens and a man in his early twenties looks at me, expectantly. Shoulder length dreadlocks are held in place by a red bandana. A gold link necklace dangles onto a muscly chest, exposed by the black vest he is wearing. He's holding a games controller, the top of which is glowing a soft red.

'Hi, I'm Detective Inspector Erika Piper,' I begin, anticipating the cold rush of air as the door is pushed towards its frame. However, it never comes. He simply keeps looking at me. 'I was wondering if you had a moment to speak.'

'I thought that's what we *were* doing,' he says, eyeing me with suspicion. He scratches the back of his neck, flexes his bicep, and I notice the Bennett Street Rebels tattoo inked on the inside of his arm.

'I was wondering if you know anything about the recent spate of murders?'

'Isn't that your job?' he spits back.

'Can I ask your name?'

'Donald.'

'Donald...'

'Duck,' he says, with a smirk.

'Okay, Donald, well that's why I'm here,' I reply, trying to keep calm. 'Can you tell me anything that might be helpful? Anything about Marcus, Kai or Charlie?'

'Nothing. They were all good people. Friends. Brothers.'

'But gang members. So, maybe, somebody out there had a reason to kill them.'

As he opens his mouth to reply, a noise from behind distracts him. He swivels his head and over his shoulder I can see a pair of very similar eyes in a younger body. The young man behind him is probably in his late teens. He is holding another controller, glowing blue, in his left hand. When he doesn't speak, I turn back to big brother.

I pull out my list and read some of the names of gang members, known to the police for previous offences. He nods at each one, a sign that he knows them, but ventures nothing. When I get to Henry Mayfield's name, big brother's body stiffens, almost imperceptibly. Little brother blurts out a strange noise, but is silenced by the look of his sibling.

'I take it you know Henry?'

He nods.

'What can you tell me about him?'

When Donald chooses not to confide in me, his little brother does.

'He lives here, but we haven't seen him in a day or two.'

I take out my notebook and fish a pen from my pocket. I open to a new page and write the date and jot down the house number. After our conversation, I'll need to check in the police database that I'm not being led on a wild goose chase.

I now focus my attention on the little brother.

'Can you be more specific?'

'He hasn't slept here for the past two nights,' he replies.

'Probably shagging about,' interrupts Donald.

I ignore him. Instead, I play on the little brother's worries. I ask for Henry's mobile number, assuring them that I will only use it for tracing purposes.

'It's not going to make any difference,' says Donald. 'I've been trying to get in touch with him, but none of my WhatsApps have even been read.'

I make a note of this information, jot down the mobile number as it is read out by the little brother and re-read it to confirm that it's correct.

'You said he was probably *shagging about*,' I say, addressing the older brother. 'Was he that type of guy?'

He shakes his head.

'Nah, it's just that he recently started going out with someone. Or so he says. We haven't met her.'

'Name?'

'Joanna.'

Something in my gut isn't sitting right. Figuratively.

'Do you mind if I look around his room?'

The older brother looks like he is about to answer negatively.

'Look,' I say. 'I want to make sure he's safe, and I'm sure you do too. Now, I can go away, sort a warrant and come back and do this. Or, you can make my life easy.'

He considers this, before somewhat reluctantly pulling open the door. I turn back to the street and shout across to Andy. I tell him that I'm following a lead in this house. He asks if I want him to come too, but I shake my head. We need to cover as many houses as we can today. There's an understanding, though, that if I'm gone for too long, he is to come and find me. Safe in the knowledge that Andy has my back, I step across the threshold.

The front room is exactly what I'd expect from a group of lads living away from the family home. Beer bottles and energy drink cans are littered around the floor. The smell of sweat mingles with the stale air, as if the windows have never been opened. Posters of women in various states of undress adorn the unevenly painted walls. An archway leads to a cramped kitchen. The lads have taken their place on the sofa again and are forming a plan on how to manoeuvre past the zombie horde on whatever shoot-em-up they are playing.

I take the stairs to the first floor and open the door to Henry's room. This room is more orderly. Perhaps Henry is the tidy one, and his absence is particularly noticeable in the clutter of downstairs. A single bed with a stripy duvet thrown over it sits along one wall. A chest of drawers with a framed picture of a blonde child on it, and a small bedside table take up the rest of the space. It really is the definition of a box room.

I pull on a pair of gloves and turn to the chest of drawers, yanking each one out. They all contain clothes that have been thrown in. There is no order. Socks and boxers are mixed with T-shirts and shorts. In one drawer, a pair of swimming goggles are tangled with a solitary stripy tie. I close the final drawer, having learned little about Henry, except that he needs to rethink his clothes storage.

The contents of the drawer on his bedside table are much more revealing. A green carrier bag contains an unopened box of condoms with a receipt, dated a few weeks ago. It seems he is not quite the ladies' man Donald believes him to be. It also suggests that, if he has got a new girlfriend, it's not her he has been spending his time with over the past two nights. A red-blooded young man would probably have tried to stuff as many of the condoms into his wallet as he could. Unless, of course, he has a separate stash of prophylactics that he keeps at her house.

I push the drawer closed and, on a whim, pull back the duvet cover. Sitting beside a pair of chequered pyjama bottoms is a mobile phone. I pick it up and press the home button, but nothing happens. I notice a charger plugged into the wall, so I shove the end of the lead into the bottom of the phone and sit on the bed, waiting. After a few minutes, the screen lights up. The home screen shows some football player—who I don't know—in a light blue T-shirt, holding a shining trophy.

Luckily, Henry is not the most security conscious. His phone unlocks without requiring a passcode. I access his calls list and find a series of names. Mostly men, except one—Mum. I navigate towards his messages and WhatsApps, and again, find a list of men's names. He seems to have a wide group of friends, and many of the conversations are either about football or arranging to go to the pub. One name jumps out.

Jack.

Jack sent the first message, on the evening that Henry was last seen, asking if they were still on for meeting up.

Yes, Henry had replied.

Cool, see you in half an hour, came Jack's reply. There, the messages had ceased.

Perhaps when the conversation had come to a close, Henry had thrown his phone down and started to get ready. Perhaps he had thrown the duvet over his phone and failed to locate it before having to leave. Maybe he left it here on purpose.

Annoyingly, this means that we cannot use his phone to trace his whereabouts. I check the calls list again for a sign of Jack's name, but it does not feature. Those three short messages are the only evidence of communication between the two. I take an evidence bag from my pocket and set the phone into it before leaving the room and making my way back downstairs.

Whatever plan they had set in motion to conquer the undead horde had obviously not worked, as they are in the same place as they were when I had left them. The younger is sat up, rigid, the controller held tight against his chest, his thumbs moving expertly over the buttons. The elder brother is much more relaxed, lying back with his head resting on the back of the sofa. When I speak, they pause the game, for fear of any distraction affecting their performance or the outcome of the plan.

'Do you know about the gang outreach meetings at the church?'

They both nod.

'Do either of you go?'

The younger brother shakes his head, whilst the elder laughs, confirming with a *fuck no* that he is not that way inclined.

'Do you know if Henry attended any meetings at the church?'

They both shake their heads at this.

'Henry is an atheist,' says the younger brother. 'When we went to the pub, he was the one who took the piss out of the ones who did go to the church. He always said there was no evidence for God's existence, and that religion was the cause of most wars.'

I make a note of this information in my pad and thank them for their time. They both see me to the door, and when I offer a card with my name and number on it, Donald steps away like it might have been laced with anthrax, while little brother moves forward to take it. The door closes behind me and as I take a few steps down the path towards the gate, I can see Andy on the other side of the street, getting another earful. When the door slams in his face, I call him back and tell him I've got a lead. I've never seen a man look more relieved in my life.

23

'SO, WHAT'S THE plan of action?' Andy asks, wiping away flecks of pastry that have caught in his stubble. He sets the pain-au-chocolat on his plate and takes a sip of his coffee.

We're currently decamped in a café, on the main road, just off Bennett Street. From our window seat, the church across the road is just visible through the steamy glass.

'Well, seeing as how we are so close to the church, I reckon we should go have a snoop about. I've already sent a picture of Henry to the office, so hopefully that'll go out soon and help us find him.'

My phone pings again; another email from another region of the country telling me they have never heard of the My Time To Die site. I'm beginning to think it's solely a local thing.

I reflect on what we know about the church. All three deceased members of the gang are confirmed as having attended the outreach program offered by the church. We know that Kenneth, the caretaker, has rather *old-fashioned* views on the finality of the gang members' fates. Though, I can't help but think his advancing years and technological prowess, or lack thereof, hold him back from using the dark web. I can't imagine him having the knowhow to set something like that up.

Which leaves Richard; the vicar, and the illusive Jack. Or, as Andy points out, any of the other members of the church. Many had voiced outrage that gangsters were allowed to come into God's house as they pleased, exasperated by Richard and Jack's ambivalence on the matter.

'So, tell me about yourself,' Andy says, as if on a first date. I give him an almost exasperated look.

'Come on,' he says, 'if we're going to be partners, we need to know a bit about each other. You know, like friends do.'

I relay brief information about my career in the police so far. I touch briefly on the facts about the stabbing and subsequent time off. For some reason, I don't want to seem vulnerable, like I'll be some sort of liability. He asks for some details about the Ed Bennett case from late last year, and I answer all of the consequent questions.

In turn, I learn a lot about him. Andy was born in Kilmarnock and attended the same school as rockers Biffy Clyro, though he was a few years younger than them. He moved to Liverpool for university and stayed in the city to join the police.

He tells me about his career to date; how he moved up the ladder, and his reasons for moving to Manchester—a city he jokingly claims he reviles, solely for footballing reasons.

'Shall we hit it, then?' he asks, grabbing his stuff and standing up.

THE FRONT DOORS of the church are locked, so we let ourselves in through the side door, left unlocked for parishioners to come and go as they please. At least, during the day. The church—devoid of bodies and seeping blood—seems much bigger than before. The silence feels almost oppressive, as if it would be rude to break it.

I take Andy on a tour of the hall as I remember it on the night the bodies were discovered. Obviously, he has read the notes and been briefed on the case so far, but having a first-hand feel of a location is very beneficial.

He listens to everything I say, before walking away and standing in the middle of the room, turning a full circle, getting a feel for the place. He walks to the door we've just come in, the one that had been blocked by Zoe's body, opens it and looks outside into the alley. It allows some warmth into the otherwise chilly room. Satisfied, he closes the door again and walks to the opposite side of the room. He tries the door, but it doesn't open. He looks in through the small, porthole style window, though the room beyond is dark due to there only being a solitary window on the far wall.

'What's in there?' he asks, as I walk towards him.

'That's the office that Richard and Jack share. When we came to the scene, that's where Richard was waiting for us. I was kind of hoping it'd be open, to get a good look around. Unsupervised.'

He looks a little surprised.

'I didn't have you down as the type to go about snooping without the correct documentation,' he says, playfully. He tries the handle again, pushing it down with more force, but still the door remains unyielding. 'The caretaker, Kenneth, has a small room in the foyer. I just want to check if it is unlocked. He seemed a bit...' I trail off.

'Weird?'

'I don't know if that's the right word, but I definitely got a bit of a strange vibe off him. He was very much in favour of the fire and brimstone God, as opposed to the forgiving, loving one. Where gang members are concerned, anyway.'

We walk to the back of the room, but before we get to the foyer, Andy takes a seat in the back pew.

'What are you doing?'

He beckons me to join him.

'Rarely, these days, and especially in this job, do you get such a peaceful moment to yourself.' He motions to the room in front of us. Stain-glassed and still.

He's right.

I sink back against the wooden pew and let the silence wash over me. I think about the difference between today's visit and the night the bodies were discovered. Teams of people, combing every inch of the room, searching for any clue at all that would help solve the case. Liam amongst them. I feel the sadness roar inside me. The injustice of it all.

Before the tears can come, I breathe in the peace of the room. I've never been religious, but there is something about this place that radiates peacefulness. I think about the little life growing inside me, and it settles me.

The stillness is broken with the opening of a door at the front of the church. Richard walks up the two steps, closes the door behind him and walks across the front of the church with something tucked under his arm. He is totally oblivious to us. When he gets to his office door, he fishes keys from the back pocket of his jeans and unlocks the door with an echoing click. He pushes it open with his shoulder and disappears.

'Wait here,' I whisper.

I leave my seat and walk back up the church, towards the front. The crucifix with Jesus' body affixed to it bears down on me, almost threateningly. The weight of his stare is overbearing. If I was a member of the congregation, I think I'd feel intimidated each week as I sat down to worship.

When I get to the door, I glance in through the porthole window. Richard is on his knees, inserting a small key into a lock next to the bottom drawer of his desk. The lock does not look like it is freely accepting his key, as he is exerting some force. Eventually, it gives, and he pulls the drawer out and places the book that was under his arm into it. Just as he is about to slide it closed, I knock.

His shoulders jerk, showing that I've startled him. He stands up at light speed and kicks the drawer closed, before calling out that I am free to enter. I push the door open and walk inside. Richard extends a hand and I shake it, noting the dampness of the palm.

'You shocked me,' he says, 'I didn't know anyone else was here.'

'I just popped in to have another look at the place,' I say. 'See if anything out of the ordinary catches my eye.'

The drawer in which the book has just been set opens slightly on its own accord. Richard seems not to have noticed.

'I couldn't help but notice that you put a book in that drawer,' I say to him, though his expression doesn't change.

'It's the prayer book,' he replies.

'What's that?'

'It's the book Jack and I use to know who to pray for and who is due a visit during the week,' he says. 'A bit like an appointment book.'

'Can I see it?'

He looks flustered. 'It's got some sensitive information. GDPR, and all that.'

I laugh. 'You do realise you are speaking to the police, don't you?'

'Of course.'

He slides the drawer out of its housing and retrieves the book, handing it to me in a fluid motion.

I flick through it. Each page of the hardback notebook is divided, a thick black line ruled along every sixth line. Each box is dedicated to a new person, though through the book, some names are repeated. Perhaps the ill and infirm that haven't made it through the particular illness or ordeal currently faced. I look at some of the names and addresses listed in the books. Margaret Surgenor had been robbed three weeks ago, and wanted the vicar to pray for her safety. A scribbled date at the side of her name confirms that Richard or Jack had visited her. The names of others are scribbled beside as well. Mandy Cookson had a recent operation and wanted to be visited in hospital. Helen Thompson, an apparently younger member of the congregation, had a recent miscarriage, and had been visited last Thursday.

Nothing in the book warrants suspicion, and I dutifully hand it back to him. He takes it from me and pops it back in the drawer, turning the key in the lock to secure it.

'Is there a similar book for the outreach program?' I ask him. I can't help but imagine how useful this would be from the police force's point of view. If we had a list of every single person who visited the church, we would have a list of potential targets. And, stretched as we would be, we could move to each address, making sure each person listed was looked after. Sadly, Richard is shaking his head.

'We were going to. But when we started asking for names, addresses and telephone numbers, the lads started kicking off. They accused us of being part of the police and hated that there was going to be a paper trail. Some walked out without a word. Jack and I thought that the main thing is that they come, so we got rid of records and the like. Sorry,' he adds, noting the disappointment on my face.

'This Jack,' I ask, waving away his apology. 'When can I meet him?'

Richard opens a desk calendar and finds today's page. He runs a finger down his assistant's side of the page, stopping his finger near the bottom.

'He's got a meeting with one of the lads from the street tonight. So, if you are here for around seven, he should be free for a chat.'

24

A BLANKET OF dark cloud has covered the summer sky, bringing with it a change in atmosphere. The usually crowded beer gardens along the busy main road near Bennett Street house only a few seasoned drinkers. The sun may not be visible, but its heat remains, bringing with it a feeling of oppression.

Andy pulls the car up on Bennett Street and puts the handbrake on. We're a little further up the street from the church.

'Are you sure you don't want me to come too?' he asks.

'I'm sure,' I nod, 'I have the beginnings of a plan in my head. You'll have to trust me.'

'You mean you do all the hard work and I get to sit in the car and read?' He holds a Kindle up. 'I think this partnership is going to work out alright!'

'Keep your radio on, just in case,' I say with a smirk. I get out of the car and close the door, giving the roof a little slap as I make my way down the street. My phone rings as I walk down the alley behind the church. When I answer it, Angela greets me. I listen to what she has to say and my breath catches in my throat. The world around me becomes blurry and I have to sit down on the low wall to stop from keeling over. I hang up and set the phone down beside me on the uneven brickwork.

Matty Richards, Liam's junkie murderer, has been caught. According to Angela, he was in a bar fight and got his ass handed to him. When the barman was picking him up off the floor, he recognised Matty from the social media campaign to catch a police killer and zip-tied him to a chair before phoning 999.

Angela had asked if I wanted to be part of his questioning, but I'd told her no. Living through it once was bad enough, twice when giving my statement had been torture. But to look into the eyes of the little fucker would be torture, and I'm not sure I could keep my cool.

Whoever was in charge of the questioning had an open and shut case. Justice would be done, and I'd make it a personal quest to find the man who broke Matty's jaw in the bar fight and buy him a beer or ten.

I close my eyes and take a few moments to compose myself. When my breathing has returned to normal, I push myself off the wall, pocket my phone and walk towards the side door, which opens with a loud click. I walk in, retracing Andy and my steps from earlier in the day, though this time I do not stop to look around, instead making my way down the aisle towards the outreach room in the church's entranceway. I knock on the door and let myself in.

Behind the door, an unexpectant Jack is sitting on a chair with a laptop balanced on his thighs, fingers moving quickly over his computer's keyboard. He greets me and apologises for not having drinks ready, explaining that his work has overrun.

He is not what I was expecting at all. As Richard's assistant, I had in mind a young lad, a twenty-something wanting to learn the ropes. Jack, on first glance, is double that. Spiky hair is held steadfastly in place with lashings of wax. Course stubble lends his face a rather dark complexion. Heavily-lidded eyes and a hooked nose contradict his hearty greeting.

He closes the lid on his laptop and sets it on the floor beside a set of keys. He rises from his chair and extends an arm. Cold, shovel-like hands close around my outstretched one whilst I introduce myself. His wide smile feels somewhat disingenuous.

'Richard told me you wanted to see me,' he says, motioning to a couple of solid wooden chairs in front of him, one of which I dutifully sink into. The small room, coupled with the seating arrangement, feels like we are in one of the police station's interview rooms. The only thing missing is a table between us.

'I just have a few questions,' I say, taking a notebook from my pocket. 'Your name has come up a few times when talking to Richard and a few of the lads on the street. I thought it would be good to put a face to the name.'

'Well,' he says, smiling. 'Here I am.'

I take a notebook out of my pocket. 'Got a surname, Jack?'

'Carter,' he replies, and I jot it down on a fresh page.

'What can you tell us about the outreach program?'

'Well,' he says, scratching the side of his head, causing a cloud of dandruff to fall. 'It was set up with only good intentions. Richard and I had seen the damage the gang culture was causing and continues to cause around here. We wanted to try and change something. So, we started putting the feelers out, trying to find out if any of the Bennett Street Rebels would come. And they did. Not in great numbers, to be honest, but in the beginning we counted even one as a win. Then, more started to turn up and by the end of the first month, we had to schedule the meetings as the numbers grew.'

'Do you see it as a success?'

He tilts his head to the side. Thinks for a minute. 'I'd say so. We've given time to lads who have been written off by society, lads who are capable of change but who have no idea how to go about making it. I think that's making a difference.'

'Did you know any of the three who were killed?'

'I knew all of them. They were mostly Richard's group, but I did know them to see. Some of the lads are more open to talking to me, some are more open with Richard.'

'Did any of the three ever disclose anything to you?'

'Yes.'

'Can you share?'

'Sorry,' he says, checking his watch, 'but the dead deserve the same respect as the living. They weren't bad lads, and they never did anything too naughty. Mostly they were involved with drugs, but they were trying to break the mould, get out of this world that they felt enslaved to. I can't say any more.'

'Do you think they would've changed their lives; had they not been murdered?'

'It's hard to say, really. Some of them seemed like they were making good progress. Some would come once and not again.'

'What about Henry?' I ask.

He sits up a little in his seat.

'What about Henry?' he repeats.

'What can you tell me about him?'

He smiles. 'It felt like Henry was here because he was being forced. The first time, he came skulking in and sat down with a face like thunder. He made it very clear that he didn't believe in God. It seemed like he wanted to provoke me. I suppose in his world that's how you assert dominance. Instead, I told him he was entitled to his opinion and asked him why he had chosen to come.'

'And why had he come?'

'He was tired of all the drama. The gang. Told me he'd had a pretty big car crash when he'd been high one night and that a promising football career had been cut short. He'd changed his aspirations, considered university instead of football.' He sighs. 'All he wanted was to get away from it all. Start again. But he didn't know how. All I could do was lend him an ear.'

'Did he say anything else?'

'He was struggling with being a father. Who can blame him at twenty-two? Anyway, when he left, he seemed unburdened. We swapped numbers and arranged to meet again.'

'But he never showed?'

He looks at me, puzzled. I tell him about finding Henry's phone and the communication between the two. Suddenly, a look of alarm flashes across Jack's face and it blanches.

'You don't think I've got anything to do with any of this, do you?' he asks, his voice wavering slightly.

'At the minute, I just need you to answer a few more questions,' I reply. Rather than tell him the truth, I reason that if I can keep him on edge, he is more likely to spill something. 'When Henry didn't show up, what did you do?'

'Well, nothing. It's not out of the ordinary for these guys to not turn up. They come here off their own back, so if they don't turn up, it just means I get to go home early.'

'Did you go home early when Henry didn't turn up?'

'Yeah.'

'Do you know he hasn't been seen, or heard from, since you messaged him?'

Again, what little colour had returned to his face fades away to white.

'I didn't know that,' is all he can manage.

'We've put out a missing persons call, so hopefully he, or someone, will come forward soon to let us know he is safe. But with what has been happening to gang members recently, it's a worrying time. Can you think of anything he might've said, any clue as to where he might be?'

He shakes his head.

'Well, if you can remember anything at all, even if it doesn't seem remotely relevant, let me know.' I hand him my card, which he takes from my grasp using his second and third finger, like a pair of scissors. He gets up to escort me to the door. Before he has a chance to take a step, I turn around and fire one more question his way.

'What makes you qualified to give advice to gang members?'

He opens his mouth to answer, but my ringtone cuts through the silence. I pull it from my pocket. The display tells me it's the police station and when I answer it, Angela's voice sounds harried.

'A body has been found matching Henry's description.'

'Let Andy know. Tell him everything he needs and we'll be there as soon as possible.'

I thank Jack for his time and make my way back to the car.

THE STORM CLOUDS that lined the sky an hour ago have disappeared, leaving a stunning crimson sky in their wake. The water in the canal behind me trickles by, the gentle lapping creating a soothing backdrop. Unfortunately, one doesn't have time to appreciate such natural beauty when faced with a decomposing body.

Henry Mayfield's bloated corpse lies on the towpath of the canal, his unseeing eyes cast towards the glowing heavens. A backpack, held to his body by two straps around his shoulders, means that he is not flat, but rather like he has been frozen mid-way through a stomach crunch. The long vest, soaked to his mottled skin, suggests that he did not leave the house with the intention of being out too long.

The section of path has been taped off and a uniformed officer stands guard at both ends. A small group of runners in black and red striped tops are using the stoppage, in what I assume must be a pre-planned route, to their advantage; some are stretching their muscles whilst others stand still, simply focusing on getting their breath back.

Already, this section of path and beyond is crawling with the forensic team—white-suited and eagle-eyed. Further down the path, I see John Kirrane making his way down the steps that lead to a car park. Having no pubs or amenities on this stretch of the canal, nor streetlights, means that this section is the perfect place to dump a body. Very little foot traffic passes by, and if someone were to disturb you, the lack of light and vast amount of overgrowing vegetation means that there are plenty of places to hide and wait it out. The nearby car-park, again unlit, is favoured by those who are usually up to no good, and would provide the opportunity of a swift getaway.

John ducks under the police tape, showing his credentials to the officer, and makes a beeline for the waiting body. He gives us a quick hello, before taking out his Dictaphone and conversing with the crime scene photographer. I know how thorough John is, and how much time this will take, so I leave him to it and approach the first responder.

'Who called it in?' I ask.

He points to a middle-aged woman who is sitting on a bench, just outside the police cordon. She clenches a mug of tea with both hands, staring at an indiscriminate spot on the gravelled ground. An excitable dog, tied to the bench by its lead, whines as I draw near. I bend down and make a fuss of him, which, after a few minutes, sates him, and he curls up on the ground at his owner's feet. I introduce myself to her, and she tells me her name is Sharon.

'Can you tell me where you found the body?' I ask, gently.

'In the canal. He was floating on the top, face down. His body was in the reeds at the side.'

'Did you see anyone else around?'

She shakes her head. 'No, it's usually very quiet around here. We live not too far away, so this is our dog walking area. In Summer, at least. I wouldn't dare venture down this way in Winter. You can't see two feet in front of you.'

'Weren't you worried about sticking around?'

Again, she shakes her head. 'Bert, here,' she points at the collie at her feet, 'is very protective.'

I think of how happy Bert was to see me, and wonder just how much of a force he would've been had the killer decided to stick around.

'Could it be The Pusher?' she asks.

I stifle a laugh. The Pusher is an urban myth around these parts. Because so many people, almost one hundred in fact, have died by drowning in the canals, it was believed that a serial killer was stalking the canal paths and using the water as a means for murder. The story has constantly been quashed by the police, and a documentary a few years ago cast further aspersions on the legend.

'We don't think so,' I say, before thanking her for her time. I assure her that any help she needs to deal with the trauma of finding a body will be organised and then walk back to the body. John is still circling the scene, though when I approach, he stops.

'What are we thinking?' I ask.

'Well, there are a few elements to this that I won't know until I complete the autopsy. What I do know is that he was subjected to a beating. The violence he sustained is obvious on his face. There's no sign of any stab or bullet wounds, so I'd say he died of either the injuries inflicted by the beating or he was drowned. Like I say, I can't be conclusive until I get a peek at his lungs.'

He looks over at Martin, the head scene of crime officer, and tells him that he is finished with the body for now. Martin summons a number of his team to perform the preliminary forensics on the immediate area surrounding the body.

'I'm assuming the tattoo suggests that a second body isn't too far behind?' John says.

I nod. 'If it's following the pattern, I'd say so.'

'Do you want me to stick around?' he asks.

I look around at the many places the body could be hidden, including the canal itself, and shake my head.

'I think it might be worth just having your phone to hand for the next twenty-four hours. Go and get some sleep.'

'And that is why I enjoy working cases with you,' he smiles, before telling us to keep him in the loop and walking away.

Andy and I hover, observing Martin and the team comb the crime scene. When they are happy that nothing has been missed in the vicinity around Henry, the backpack is removed and the body is lifted into a bag, and then onto a stretcher, and carried up the steps to a waiting vehicle. Martin bends down and instructs the photographer to take a number of pictures of the backpack.

The faded blue material and the peeling Adidas logo make the bag look old. Of course, that could have something to do with it being submerged in filthy canal water for an unspecified amount of time. The zips, which have been pulled up from either side of the bag to meet in the middle, are parted slightly. Martin swabs the outside and then unzips the bag, removing a number of rocks and placing each one in an evidence bag, though he and I both know that they will almost certainly be of no use to us.

Inside, stitched into the back panel, is a name tag, though it has mostly disintegrated. All that is left are the final five letters of the surname –CETTE, presumably belonging to the person who owned the bag. And, therefore, possibly belonging to the killer.

I ring Angela, who has remained at the station, and ask her to search the database for any names containing CETTE which could have any kind of link to the case. She assures me that she's on it, and will send through anything worth looking at. When I hang up, I call Martin over and voice my theory about the second body, lying in wait at the bottom of the canal. He pulls out his phone and makes a call. He has a quick-fire conversation with whoever is on the other end, before telling me that he can have a dive team here in two hours' time. I okay it and he confirms, before shoving the phone back into his pocket.

I consider calling it a day. The dive team won't be here for a couple of hours and Martin will keep me informed if a body is found. For some reason, Liam flashes into my mind. I imagine him standing on the banks of the canal; his keen eyes taking in every detail, hungry for justice. He'd shake his head at me and call me a part-timer if I'd chosen to head home on his watch. I rebuke myself for even considering it at such a crucial time in the case.

As if operating on the same wavelength, Andy walks to a bench within the confines of the police tape. He sits down and taps the seat beside him. When I join him, he asks me to go over the case again, from the very start. I admire his commitment and his will to get to the bottom of all of this. Again, I admonish myself for being such a dick to him on his first day.

We go through the case from the beginning and he jots down names, places and other pertinent details. When we are finished discussing the case and awaiting the arrival of the divers, we chat like friends would. He tells me more about his family and I tell him more about me. Guilt gnaws at my stomach each time I laugh, as if my growing fondness of him is somehow lessening my love of Liam. I try to think rationally, though the gut reaction doesn't follow suit and I find myself closing off. I become less chatty. I put in less effort until an awkward silence comes between us. I make an excuse and walk to the water's edge, pretending to peer in.

I'm saved by the sound of vehicles entering the car park at the top of the steps. A few minutes later, a group of divers dressed in dry suits and carrying heavy breathing apparatus appear. I brief them on what we are looking for while heavy duty spotlights are set up. One of the divers laughs at the futility of the light, insisting that they won't make a blind bit of difference below the water's surface.

When they are ready, they lower themselves into the canal and assume a formation, before submerging themselves. A group of officers on the bank keep them in line and ensure their safety. Andy and I stand back near the bench, in order to keep out of the way.

After a period of time, the length of canal separated from the rest by police tape has been searched by the divers, yielding plenty of rubbish, but no body. The lead officer tells me that they can keep going, though he doubts that the flow of water is substantial enough to move a body weighed down by a backpack of stones. I trust his judgement so we call it.

As the divers pull themselves out of the water, alarm bells ring in my head. There are now two scenarios. Henry Mayfield was killed by someone unrelated to the case. Or, more likely, whoever orchestrated the killings of Marcus, Kai and Charlie has decided to take matters into their own hands.

25

I WAKE WITH a start and immediately register the heaviness of my eyes. I'm not surprised, given how little sleep I'd managed to fit in last night. I check my phone and notice that Angela has sent through a small list of potential suspects with '—CETTE' name matches. I throw the phone onto Tom's empty side of the bed, the case the last thing on my mind this morning. I roll out of bed and head to the shower. As the water washes over me, I think about Liam. Today is his funeral, a day I've been dreading. Until now, it's almost like he has just been on holiday, enjoying his honeymoon on some far-flung beach in the Pacific. But, today, I will watch his body lowered into a hole in the ground, and everything will be final. He will be gone, and I will have to accept that. As this idea rears its head, tears stream from my eyes and mingle with the warm water.

When I enter the kitchen, a besuited Tom is sitting at the table, looking how I feel; a slice of buttery toast going cold on the plate in front of him. He gives me a little smile as I walk in and tells me he likes the dress I have chosen. I consider breakfast, but my stomach feels as though it has turned itself inside out. I take a small sip of Tom's orange juice and then we leave the house.

THE METHODIST CHURCH which Liam's parents still attend is an impressive building. Outside, beautiful stonework and an impressively tall bell tower lend the church a rather medieval feel. Despite arriving early, the car park is already full, with some attendees having abandoned their vehicles on grass verges on the roadside. If Liam were here, he'd be shaking his head disapprovingly and considering doling out some parking tickets. As it is, they will go unpunished.

Tom takes my hand as we enter the building. The church is smaller than the one on Bennett Street. There is no entranceway. Instead, the doors lead straight into the main room. Dark, wooden pews stretch from front to back in two banks. Intricate stained-glass windows depict some of the Bible's famous stories; Jesus feeding the five thousand, Jonah and the whale, and Noah sailing the waves on his celebrated ark laden with animals.

Despite the beauty, my eyes are drawn to the wooden coffin at the front of the room and a sob catches in my throat. Tom squeezes my hand.

'Do you want to see him?' he asks.

I nod, and we navigate our way through the quiet crowd, making our way to Liam. A small line has formed, and each person takes a minute or two—a final moment with their friend.

The last time I saw Liam, I'd held him as he'd bled out and died with his head on my thigh. I'd held him long after he'd taken his final breath. I wonder if the gash where the blade carved through his neck like it was made of soft butter will be visible and what will happen to me if it is. When the sobbing woman in front of me walks away, I take a step forward and brace myself.

The team in charge of Liam's autopsy and subsequent care has done an impeccable job. He is wearing a smart, black suit with a pink shirt and a paisley tie; the one from his wedding. A final outfit I think he'd be pleased with. His hair is as short as it's ever been, and the peaceful look on his face gives me some hope that he didn't have to suffer for long. The shirt collar covers the entry point of the knife. If I hadn't known how he'd died and I was told he died peacefully in his sleep, I'd have believed it. I reach in and hold his cold hand in mine. After a minute, I relinquish my grasp and, with it, my last physical connection to a colleague; a friend who was more like a brother.

The church is heaving with bodies; a testament to Liam's popularity. A lot of the crowd is made up of work friends, past and present. There's a huddle of men I don't recognise—some with scrapes on their faces and cauliflower ears, who I assume were his rugby teammates.

The priest, grey and hunched, walks slowly up the aisle and those who were standing around, swapping stories, take this as their cue to find a seat.

The priest begins the ceremony by welcoming us. His tone is solemn but there is a twinkling in his eyes. He tells us that conducting a funeral is never easy, but it is made somewhat harder when the deceased are taken in their prime. He regales the assembled crowd with stories of Liam; his first day of Sunday school, the time he managed to steal a sip of wine during communion, aged eight. As the stories continue, I can see a few people's shoulders in the front row rise and fall. A few Bible passages are read out and a prayer is offered, and then my name is called. A few days ago, Dylan had phoned me and asked if I would speak at the ceremony. In the intervening time, I'd tried to write something, but everything sounded like Hallmark had written it for one of their cards. In the end, I'd decided to do it off the cuff.

I walk to the pulpit and look out at the crowd. I can feel my knees wobble. I take a deep breath and begin.

'Liam was a great man and a great friend. I was only lucky enough to know him for four years or so, but I feel like I've known him a lifetime. I'm sure that feeling is shared by many of us here.'

There is a ripple of agreement which emboldens me.

'Liam was many things. A fantastic police officer, a loving husband, a son, a brother, but above all else he was a decent human being. In his final moments,' I stop, and take another breath. I can feel the tears well in my eyes. 'In his final moments, he told me I was going to be a good mum. He cared more about me in that moment than himself, and that, for me, sums him up. I will miss him forever, but I count myself very lucky that I was blessed enough to know him for the time I did.'

The silence that follows is deafening. I can feel the blood rush in my ears as I make my way towards my seat. Liam's mum holds out an arm and I hold her hand momentarily. When I take my seat, Tom shifts a little closer and holds me. I can feel the adrenaline flood my body and the tears and emotion I have so far been holding back come to the fore. I'm not the only one.

The mood soon changes when some of the rugby lads take to the front. They tell more upbeat stories about Liam on nights out and funny incidents on the rugby pitch. By the end of the ceremony, the mood feels celebratory, and I know that is what he would've wanted.

When the priest has finished his final blessing, the pallbearers pick the coffin up and walk down the aisle. The crowd rises and follows them slowly to the graveside. The grave has been dug in the family plot, next to one of his grandfathers. A short prayer is said before Liam is lowered into his final resting place. A number of people throw in a handful of dirt and make their way back inside, towards the church hall; towards the buffet.

When the crowd has gone, I notice Dylan by the graveside. He bends down and mutters something towards the partially covered coffin and a little grin spreads across his face. It feels perverse, almost voyeuristic to watch such an intimate moment, so I turn away. As I'm make my way up the hill towards the church, I hear my name. When I spin around, I see that Dylan is walking towards me.

'Sorry for your loss,' I say to him.

'And I'm sorry for yours,' he replies. 'We all said goodbye to someone special today.'

I nod and let out a sniffle.

Dylan reaches into his inside jacket pocket and retrieves an A4 envelope that has been folded in half.

'I found this in Liam's study. I think it's something about the current case as I recognised the name Richard. It could be nothing though.'

He hands me the envelope, which I slip into my handbag, and we walk up the slope and round the front of the church. He hugs me before walking through the door towards the food. I approach the priest to thank him for conducting the ceremony on behalf of the police force. We shake hands and talk about Liam for a little while. As the conversation is coming to a close, he mentions the current case.

'I hear there are some goings on at St Peters.'

I'm somewhat taken aback, though, of course, information about the case has been reported in the press.

'Yes. We attended a crime scene there last week.'

He looks sad. 'In the Lord's house, of all places. You'd think people would have some respect. I just hope Nicolo has nothing to do with this.'

'Nicolo?' I ask. So far, Nicolo is not a name that has come up in the investigation.

'Ah, of course, you might know him as Jack. When he got out of prison, he changed his name. New name, new start. Of course, he'll always be little Nicolo to me. He started coming to church when he was just a little boy. He'd have been about ten years older than Liam. He went off the rails in his late teens. Became involved in a gang and got himself into trouble. He went to prison for GBH in his twenties. When he got out, he came to see me, apologised for what he had done and asked me not to let it affect my perception of his family. He told me he had changed his name to Jack Carter and was looking to get into ministry; to help change the lives of others.'

'So he was Nicolo Carter when you knew him?' I ask.

'No,' he says, 'the family name is Salvicette.'

My mouth drops open. He smiles sadly at me and asks if I am going to the buffet. I tell him that, unfortunately, I have somewhere to be.

I run up to Tom and tell him what I have just learned. It comes out as a stream of consciousness and I can see that he isn't following.

'The bag we found last night, attached to the drowned boy, had a fragment of a name tag –CETTE. I've just found out that assistant priest Jack Carter's real name is actually Nicolo Salvicette.'

'Fuck,' he mutters, a little too loudly for a church setting, and receives a number of tuts from a few of the elderly funeral-goers gathered nearby. 'Go on. Go.'

26

I RUN INTO my office and throw myself into my chair, logging onto the police database in record time. When it loads, I type in Nicolo Salvicette's name and am amazed at the length of his rap sheet.

In his teens and twenties, Nicolo amassed a wide range of convictions—drug dealing, anti-social behaviour and robbery. He'd been in and out of prison, serving short stints here and there, before a three-year stretch for committing grievous bodily harm—on his father, no less—that must've been the one that scared him straight. After that, his criminal record comes to an end.

I'd really love to believe that, in this case, the prison system worked. That the time and money spent on rehabilitating Nicolo Salvicette had a lifelong effect. But the criminal record, coupled with the fact that he withheld name change information, casts a rather large spotlight on him. Not to mention the tag in the rucksack.

I summon Andy to my room and tell him of my intentions for the day, and he agrees to come with me.

WE PARK ON Bennett Street and make our way down towards the church. It feels like a second home at the minute, and I find myself hoping that this will be the last time I have to visit here, that today's findings will close the case. We let ourselves in the side door and walk across to the office, where Jack is sitting on a swivel chair, writing in a notebook. When we knock, he swivels around and shouts come in. When we open the door, he seems surprised to see us.

'Jack, we need you to come to the station for another chat,' I say.

'OK,' he says. 'Anything I can do to help.'

The coolness of his answer is cancelled out by the beads of sweat on his forehead. He moves to put the notebook in the drawer, but I stop him.

'Is that your prayer book?'

'Well, not mine, but the one Richard and I share.'

'Would you mind bringing that with you?'

He shrugs his shoulders, mumbles an agreement and stands up. We walk out of the office and out through the side door. As we direct him to our car, he tells us that he has left his wallet in his car and that it is parked in the church car park. I worry that he is going to drive away, so we follow him down the alley towards the little car park. He holds up his keys and presses a button, causing a car's lights to flash near the back wall. The car in question is a metallic orange sports car with a black spoiler.

'Is this your car?' I ask.

'Yes,' he beams with pride. 'Since I was little, I've always wanted an Evo.'

I close the gap between us with a few steps. 'Jack Carter, you are under arrest for the murders of Marcus Sharpe, Clive Burston, Kai McCormick, Zoe Sullivan, Charlie Hill and Henry Mayfield. You are also under arrest for the attempted murder of Manon Marchand.'

I take the prayer book from him, then proceed to read him his rights as Andy cuffs him. His protests fall on deaf ears as we lead him to the police car.

It's almost seven o'clock by the time the interview with Jack begins. He claims he has nothing to hide as he has done nothing wrong, so has declined the offer of legal representation. The good-natured attitude I'd experienced from Jack on our previous meeting has gone. Now, he sits sullenly on the other side of the table in the small interrogation room, an elbow resting on the table.

I press the button on the recording device and DCI Bob speaks first. 'Commencing interview with Jack Carter. Present are Detective Chief Inspector Bob Lovatt and Detective Inspector Erika Piper. Interview conducted at 18:57 on Thursday the fourteenth of August 2019. Jack has declined the offer of legal representation.'

'Jack,' I start, taking over from Bob, 'or should I call you Nicolo? Can you please tell us why you didn't think to mention your change of name?'

His eyes widen. 'Honestly, I thought if you found out about my past, you'd put two and two together and get five. I assume you've looked at my list of convictions?'

I nod.

'Who I am now is not who I was then,' he states.

'Can you see how it looks bad on you that you didn't mention it?'

'I do,' he confirms. 'But like I said, I didn't think it was important to the case.'

'Why did you beat your father half to death?' I ask.

He sighs. 'My dad was not the upstanding citizen everyone thought he was. He was a church goer and a local businessman and was keen to keep that facade. Behind closed doors, he was a right mean bastard.'

'So, why did you attack him?'

'I was high. I went to their house to grab some clothes that mum had washed for me. He accused me of stealing and grabbed me by the throat. It was one time too many. I threw him off me and the red mist descended. When I realised what I'd done, I ran.'

He is trying to keep calm, but there is a slight tremble in his voice that tells me it is taking a lot of effort. Old habits die hard. I take a photograph of the bag that was filled with stones and attached to Henry Mayfield's body and set it on the table.

'Do you recognise this bag?' I ask.

He glances at the photo and confirms that he does.

'Is it yours?'

'No,' he answers. 'It belongs to my nephew.'

'And how did it end up at the crime scene, filled with rocks?'

He shrugs his shoulders. 'Beats me.'

'Where did you last see it?'

'I keep it as a spare school bag for Luca, usually in the boot of my car. My sister is an alcoholic and therefore fairly unreliable, so some of the time I take Luca to give him some stability.'

'And did you notice the bag was missing?'

'I did actually,' he nods. 'But sometimes he takes it home by mistake, or forgets to bring it home from school.'

'And you keep it in the boot of this car?' I ask, emphasizing the *this* as I slide a second picture onto the table. This picture is the CCTV still, showing Jack's car chasing mine on the night Manon was shot.

'Yes, that's my car.'

'So, this is you, chasing after us and firing three gunshots through our window?'

Confusion contorts his face.

'I've never fired a gun in my life. Not even during my darker days. And certainly not last week,' he says, pointing to the date stamp in the bottom corner of the photograph.

'Are you claiming that this is not you driving your car?'

'That's what I'm saying.'

'So,' I ask, 'who is it?'

'Richard,' he replies.

'And why is Richard driving your car?' DCI Bob asks.

'Because he asked if he could borrow it for a few days. His is a shit heap and had trouble starting, and he had visits to do, so he asked could he use mine.'

Jack leans back in his chair and looks exhausted. I take the momentary lapse in questioning to try and make sense of what he has just told us. The evidence against him is damning; the name change, his past, his nephew's bag and his car. But, if he is telling the truth about lending his car to Richard, it changes everything. For now, until I speak to Richard, Jack is still my prime suspect.

I tell Bob that I will be back in a minute, and get up to leave. When I am in my office, I navigate through the phone book on my mobile and find Richard's number. I dial it on the station's handset. He answers very quickly, like he was holding the phone in his hand already.

'Richard, it's DI Erika Piper. I have a quick question if that's okay?'

'Fire away,' he replies.

'Have you ever driven Jack's car?'

There's a moment of silence on the other end.

'Yes,' he replies eventually. 'I've moved it in the car park once or twice if he was blocking the exit, but other than that, no. You've seen my car. I don't think I could handle his rocket.' He trails off with laughter.

'Odd,' I say, 'because we're questioning him at the minute in relation to the murders and he is blaming you.'

I'm hoping that this will put the cat amongst the pigeons and set his tongue wagging. And it does. Quite spectacularly.

'Not surprising,' he says. 'To be honest, he has been acting strange lately. Do you know about his past?'

I tell him I do.

'Well, he's been very secretive about who he is meeting with and is on his laptop an awful lot. He never used to bring it to work, but now he does, and anytime I walk in on him, he closes the lid. I began to worry about whether he was involved, but convinced myself that he really did leave Nicolo behind. That Jack was an honourable man. Are you telling me he is behind all this nastiness?'

'That's what we are trying to ascertain now. Thank you for your time, Richard.'

'Not at all, love,' he says. 'If I can do anything else, please let me know.'

I hang up and walk back towards the interview room. When I enter, I sit down beside Bob and shake my head. Bob's gentle voice takes me by surprise.

'Look, son, here's where we are. My best friend was one of the first to die in this mess. At the minute, I am holding you personally responsible for his death, and the others, and will be pushing for the maximum prison sentence possible. I, personally, will ensure that you never see the light of day again. I'd suggest you get a lawyer before we question you further. Is that something we can help you with?'

He nods his head. Bob throws his chair back and leaves the room.

'Someone will be with you shortly to escort you to a cell for the evening,' I tell a scared looking Jack, before following Bob out of the room.

I'm ready to die. Please help me.

This is what I type into the private chat with The Guide on the My Time To Die website. If Jack is the mastermind behind all of this, then there won't be a reply. If there is a reply, it proves that Jack is innocent and that it is someone else. Unless Jack is working as part of a team.

I log out of the website and close down the computer, before heading home for the night, ready for an early start in the morning.

I pour myself a glass of water in the kitchen and flick the lights off. As I make my way through the living room towards the stairs, I notice the handbag I'd taken to the funeral, discarded on the sofa alongside Tom's suit jacket and wallet. I sit down and open the bag, taking the brown envelope that Dylan had handed me.

Inside are a number of sheets of paper. Some are printed screenshots of pages from the internet and some are handwritten. I feel my heart jolt as I realise that this scrawled writing is a little physical connection to Liam. I trace his writing with my finger before holding the pages to my nose; the familiar smell of his favourite aftershave fills my nostrils. My eyes begin to blur with tears, so I move the paper away, mindful not to let my waterworks drip onto the pages.

When I get my emotions under control, I pick the papers up and look at what he'd been up to. It seems that he had been researching Richard's past life in his spare time. There are many different avenues that he has explored, but the one that jumps out to me is that Richard's biological father—Bernard Clark—was killed in a gangland fight. His dead body was found alongside another. My mind immediately jumps to our current bout of murder-suicides, and I wonder if this was an early incantation. At this stage, it's purely speculative though. Richard told us he had no knowledge of his birth parents' whereabouts, or even if they were still alive.

The plan I had dreamt up changes slightly in my head, and I'm keen to put it into practice, but I know that with Jack in custody and the weight of the day, I need to sleep. I make my way upstairs and turn the light off. I'm asleep before I hit the pillow.

WHISPERS IN THE DARK

27

WHEN I LOG onto the My Time To Die site the next morning, I'm unsurprised to find out that I have not received a reply to my message. I exit out of the private conversation and check various forums, but there is no sign of any participation from The Guide. I log out again and prepare to head to the station.

Shortly after ten o'clock, the questioning of Jack Carter begins again. This time, with a lawyer beside him. His lawyer does most of the talking and it's obvious that he has spent the night learning every facet of the case, and the accusations levelled at his new client.

He agrees that not supplying us with the name change information looks bad, but argues that Luca Salvicette's bag at the crime scene is circumstantial. He also praises Jack's selflessness and community spirit in lending his car to Richard so that church visits could still go ahead. When I inform them that Richard denies this, the lawyer claims that there is no way of proving who was driving, therefore it is Richard's word against Jack's. He has an answer for everything and Bob becomes quickly frustrated.

'You've got,' the lawyer says, making a show of pulling his sleeve up and consulting a very expensive timepiece on his wrist, 'just under nine hours until my client has to be released, so...'

'We're letting him go now,' I interrupt.

Jack looks confused whilst the lawyer looks triumphant. I can only imagine how much he has been paid for the relatively small amount of work he has had to do. I can feel Bob bristle next to me, but he doesn't say a word.

'Someone will be with you soon to sort you out before you leave,' I tell Jack, before shaking his and his lawyer's hand and leaving the room. Bob grunts an unfriendly goodbye and, as we leave, whispers that he wants to see me in his office.

When he has stalked around his desk and thrown himself into his chair, he fixes me with a steely glare.

'What the fuck are you thinking?' he barks.

'We need proof,' I say. 'And we are not going to get it from him with him sitting in a holding cell.'

I tell him my plan, involving the My Time To Die forum. How I have already made contact with The Guide and how I plan to use the chatroom to bring the culprit into the open; to drag him out from behind the safety of a computer screen. Bob agrees that the plan has legs, but tells me not to put myself in danger. He looks at my stomach when he says it, and I remember that it is not just me who I have to keep safe now. He tells me to keep him in the loop and then excuses me.

As I am walking back to my office, my mobile phone vibrates in my pocket. I close the door behind me and answer the incoming call.

'Erika, how are you?' asks John Kirrane.

'I'm very well,' I reply. 'How are you?'

'I'm well too,' he confirms. 'Sorry I couldn't be at the funeral yesterday. I hope you held up OK.'

I thank him for his kindness.

'I've been busy with Henry's body,' he says, moving onto business. 'Hopefully what I have for you will be helpful.'

'Go on.'

'He died from massive trauma to the brain, it was severely swollen. His lungs were clear of water, so he was already dead when he hit the canal. It seems the killer simply wanted the body hidden. It would also seem that since I haven't received a second body, that one has not been found.'

I tell John about the fruitless search of the canal.

'Ok, keep me informed if anything crops up. I'll send Henry's report across as soon as it has been typed up. See you later, Erika.'

I hang up and put my phone back in my pocket. I open up my notebook and find a new page. I scribble down what John has just told me. Henry's Bennett Street Rebels tattoo was blatantly on display on his body, so the obvious thing to think is that a second body will turn up and the two deaths can easily be connected. But, if it doesn't, and it is looking more and more unlikely, Henry's murder doesn't fit with the killer's modus operandi. All the other crime scenes have been in fairly obvious places, waiting to be discovered. The fact that whoever did this tried to hide the body makes me think again about the possibility that Henry was killed by someone unconnected to the case, though this still seems far too much of a coincidence. The more obvious explanation is that whoever is behind the keyboard acting as The Guide has stepped out and got their own hands dirty. Which means Henry must've had some sort of connection to the killer.

I ball my fist in frustration. The answer to all of this seems so close, yet it feels that I can't join the dots. I write down a list of the gang members who have been killed so far—Marcus Sharpe, Kai McCormick, Charlie Hill, and Henry Mayfield—trying to find connections between them that aren't there. Eventually, I slam my pen down on the desk.

My attention is drawn to the outer office, where Jack and his lawyer are walking towards the lifts, towards freedom. The lawyer walks with a gait that looks like his thighs are rubbing together uncomfortably, and Jack has a look of deep relief on his face. They make an odd couple. I wonder if I am watching a killer leave, a killer that I have freed on a wild theory that he is going to give himself up via a dodgy internet chatroom.

As I am about to get up to make a drink, in the hope that some ice-cold water will stir my brain into action, perhaps encourage it to investigate an avenue not yet explored, my phone vibrates again and I am surprised to see that it is my sister calling.

'Hi, sis, everything OK?' I answer.

'Erika, don't panic, but dad has had a fall. They think he has broken his hip. We're in an ambulance on the way to Stepping Hill.'

I can hear Dad grumbling in the background about making a fuss over nothing and that he doesn't need a welcoming party at the hospital. I assure Sarah that I will be there and hang up.

'Dad has had a fall, I'm just heading to the hospital,' I call around Bob's door before heading towards the lift. As I am waiting for the lift to reach my floor, I nip back to my office and pick up the prayer book Jack has left behind. I keep picturing Richard placing it carefully in the drawer before locking it, and wondering if I am missing something significant within its pages. I reason that if there is some spare time at the hospital, I can use it wisely. With the book in my hand, I make my way to the car.

I PULL INTO the car park and find a space. Sarah doesn't answer when I try to ring her, so I get out and walk into the main reception area. It's as busy as ever, and I imagine how annoyed dad will be, thinking that he is wasting the time of a doctor or nurse who could be helping someone in real need. I pull my phone out again, just to check that Sarah hasn't attempted to call me back. She hasn't.

I find a vacant chair and squeeze in beside a man dressed in a green stripy football kit, who winces as he shifts a swollen ankle, and a crying woman with a badly burnt forearm, whose husband is trying to console her.

I open the prayer book and look through it from the start. The entries in this book begin at the start of March, and I assume it is one of many prayer books that have been used throughout the years. Each entry has a name, a date, and a reason they have requested a visit or a prayer. I scan through, though I have no idea what I am looking for. Then, a fragment of a conversation with Jack emerges. He said that Henry came once, a week before his no-show. He also said that they stopped recording entries for the gang members. Perhaps Jack had stopped recording their visits, but

Richard hadn't. The messy handwriting is that of Richard's. Maybe, when Jack and Richard were discussing meetings, Richard took to recording them for some reason.

I flip the pages forward to early August and search for Henry Mayfield's name, but it isn't there. However, there is a Helena McMullan. Her entry states that she crashed into another car and failed to stop. The entry is also the only one on the page that has been highlighted in luminous yellow. This sounds suspiciously like the crime Henry confessed to during his meeting with Jack. I flip backwards through the book, searching for the names of the other gang members who have died, but again, their names are not there. I do however find a Margaret Stone, a Keira Magnussen and a Ciara Hooper. Their entries have not been highlighted, but the dates fit with when the stricken gang members would have visited. I flip forward to Helena's entry again and re-read it. My stomach drops.

The memory of being in Richard's home comes flooding back. Just as we were leaving, we had discussed how his wife and child had died in a car crash; a car crash the police told him had been a joyriding accident. Richard had seemed blasé about it, stating that it was in God's plan and that the Almighty moved in mysterious ways.

But now it strikes me that Richard didn't believe that for a second. It might've been in God's plan, but what if Richard's plan was to seek revenge on the man who tore his family apart? Just as the revelation comes crashing down around me, a shout from reception makes me jump. I look up to see an elderly gentleman has fallen and is lying face down on the floor.

Today seems to be the day for falls. Two middle-aged men, probably his sons, grasp him under his armpits, trying to raise him to a standing position. Behind the desk, the receptionist with the flame red hair, who was working when I came to visit Manon, asks if she can help, though both sons shake their heads. I have a sudden thought and approach the reception desk.

'Can I help you?' she asks as I reach her. The tag on her chest states that her name is Rebecca.

'Yes,' I reply. 'This is going to sound strange, but do you know Richard Clark? He's a priest.'

She nods.

'He's in here all the time visiting patients. He's a lovely man.'

'He seemed annoyed the other day when you wouldn't let him visit one of his congregation.'

She looks confused for a second, before seemingly remembering the incident I'm referring to.

'How do you know about that?' she asks.

'I was here visiting someone connected to the case I'm currently investigating. I bumped into him as I was leaving and he seemed angry. When I asked him why, he told me he was refused entry to someone who was expecting him.'

'Ah, well, that's not quite the truth,' she says. 'He was asking to see someone who was brought in the night before. He was quite insistent that she was expecting him, but I'd been told by one of the police officers not to let any visitors in to see her.'

My heart is racing.

'Do you remember her name?' I ask.

'No, I know it was French… give me a second,' she pushes herself away from the desk and flicks through a filing cabinet. She grabs a file from it and wheels her way back to the desk. 'Manon Marchand.'

'Is she still here?' I ask.

'No, it says here she was discharged two days ago.'

I thank her for her time and race out the door.

ON MY WAY back to my house, I make three phone calls. The first is to DCI Bob, explaining what I have just uncovered in the prayer book and from the hospital receptionist. I tell him that the plan is still on, the plan to bring Richard out into the open. He agrees and tells me to let him know when it is go time.

The second phone call is to my sister, explaining that there has been a massive breakthrough on the case and that I will visit dad as soon as humanly possible. The third and final phone call is to Andy, telling him to get his ass to my house as quickly as he can.

When I get in the door, I get my laptop from the drawer and log onto the dark web and click onto the My Time To Die website. I discover that I have a private message waiting for me. I click onto the thread that displays the messages sent so far. I begin to type and am pleased to see that The Guide is online too as the messages come quickly. We converse for a short period of time, and the conversation quickly takes a turn for the sinister.

There is a knock on the door that scares the life out of me, but when I peek out of the window, I see Andy, who is drumming a rhythm on his leg. I open the door and let him in. I lead him to the laptop and show him the conversation so far. He reads it with widening eyes.

ME
I'm ready to die. Please help me.
THE GUIDE
Forgive me for the late reply, I was tied up last night
If you still want to die, I can help.
ME
I'm ready.
THE GUIDE
Tonight?
ME
Yes.
THE GUIDE
If I am going to help you, I need you to do something for me.
ME

Anything
THE GUIDE
I need you to kill for me.
In the same way you will kill yourself.
I will set everything in motion.
The one you are to kill will be waiting for you.
They will be bound, so there will be no struggle.
A gun will be provided.
All you need to do is shoot them. Once in the back of
the head. And then again.
Once you have shot them, you shoot yourself. Once
under the chin.
Nothing will be left to chance.
ME
I only want to kill myself.
I don't want to harm anyone else.
THE GUIDE
In that case, I cannot help you.
ME
Why do I need to kill someone?
THE GUIDE
I do not need to explain myself.
Either you want my help.
Or you don't.
ME
I do want your help.
Have they done something bad?
THE GUIDE
Yes, something terrible. But I cannot tell you what.
Come to St Peter and The Light Methodist church.
Tonight.
7pm.
Your victim and your way out of this life will be waiting.
ME

Thank you so much for helping me.
Can I at least know the victim's name?
THE GUIDE
Her name is Erika Piper.
I will make sure she is there.
Goodbye.

'Fuck,' he says, pushing the laptop away from him and locking eyes with me. I fill him in with what I have found out today, about the clues that led me to finding out that Richard is the mastermind behind all this bloodshed. I begin to explain my plan to him, but I'm interrupted by a ringing in my pocket.

'Here he is now, luring me to my death,' I say, pulling the phone from my pocket. When I look at the screen though, my certainty that Richard is behind all of this vanishes.

Jack's name flashes on the screen.

'Hi Jack, how can I help you?'

'Erika, I've just thought of something that I think links Richard to the killings. Can we meet at the church later on tonight?'

'Can't you tell me over the phone?' I ask.

'I'd prefer to do it face to face.'

'What time?'

'Six thirty,' he says, before hanging up.

28

'YOU'RE SURE YOU know every detail of the plan?'

'For the millionth time, yes,' Andy replies. He may be being flippant, but he and I are both aware of the many risks involved with my idea. If all goes well, by the end of the night we will have a confession and the killer in custody. I check the time and realise that unless I leave in the next couple of minutes, I'm going to be late.

Confusion has reigned in the past few hours since Jack's phone call. Either Jack called because he has information pertinent to the case, or he really is the mastermind behind My Time To Die. The Guide said he would organise it so that I was at the church before 'Joseph' turned up, and so far, the only contact I have had is from Jack.

But, if Jack is the killer, why was Richard so angry at not being allowed access to Manon? Perhaps he was trying to get to her, having discovered Jack's plan, to apologise? Or maybe Richard and Jack are working together. It's a thought that hadn't really occurred to me before. It must be difficult to organise so much on your own, and even harder to keep one's shenanigans a secret. It makes sense that they would trust each other. Either way, the plan that is about to unfold will bring the killer—or killers—out into the open.

Andy and I walk out of my flat and get into our respective cars. He gives me a nod, and in that moment, I trust him completely. I know he's got my back. As he reverses out of the driveway, I call Bob and tell him that the operation is about to begin.

'I don't think you should do it,' he says over the loudspeaker. 'I'm calling it off.'

'Why?' I ask, incredulous that he is changing his mind at the last minute. 'It's time to catch the killer.'

'Last time you went into a building trying to save someone, it very nearly ended your life. And now, you've got more than your own life to think about.'

'I know the risks,' I say. 'The other bodies, aside from Henry, were drugged, orally, from what John said. We know that at the outreach meetings Jack and Richard provided bottles of water, so it makes sense that the bottle is laced with whatever they were using. I'm going to pretend to drink the water, Andy will knock on the door, pretending to be Joseph and we arrest whoever is behind this. No-one gets hurt.'

There is silence as Bob considers the plan.

'Okay. We go ahead. But I'm sending extra officers to contain the area and Andy needs to get there at bang on the right fucking second.'

I PULL INTO the church car park and manoeuvre the car in between Jack's sports car and Richard's rusty estate. I get out and take in my surroundings. The sky is a kaleidoscope of purples and pinks and I am awed by its beauty. I think of the people that the My Time to Die website is targeting and bile rises in my throat. The vulnerable side of society should be getting help with living, not with dying.

I walk down the alleyway and push on the side door I feel like I've used too often to gain access to this church. This time the door is unyielding. I don't knock, for fear of giving away my whereabouts before I need to. I realise that even though there is a plan in place to obtain a confession, and even though you can forecast most variables, there is always risk of a spanner in the works.

'Can you hear me?' I whisper into my radio.

'Loud and clear,' comes an immediate reply from Andy.

I move around the outside of the church and come to the front entrance. Inside, there is no sign of life, though the doors separating the foyer from the main room are open.

The smell of dust on a hot day greets me as I enter the building; a musty smell, telling me that the cleaners haven't been in for a few days. The colourful flowers on the vestibule table are drooping over the side of the vase, in desperate need of water. A handful of neatly stacked leaflets and a well-stocked food basket for a local homeless charity take up much of the remaining space.

I step past the basket and peek into the main room. Sunlight flows in through the windows, casting coloured patterns on the dark wooden pews. In my head, I was expecting some sort of elaborate welcome, but the church remains as tranquil and hallowed as ever. I take a few quiet steps into the room, and sense movement behind the door to my left. As I turn in the direction of the disturbance, an almighty blow lands on the side of my head. My vision immediately blurs and I can feel warm blood begin to flow freely down my face. I fall to my knees and my world becomes awash with blackness.

I WAKE UP with water being splashed in my face. The first thing I notice is that my gun has been removed from my belt. I can feel the imbalance of weight on my thighs. I open my eyes, slowly at first; narrow slits to try and make out where I am. The blinding pain in my head stops my eyes from opening any further anyway.

I try and move my hand up to my face, to wipe away some of the water that clings to my eyelashes, but realise that I have been bound to a hard-backed chair. Though the pain is almost overwhelming, I force my eyes open a fraction more and look up into the face of Richard.

'Not who you were expecting?' he asks. His words reach my ears in fragments, and my battered brain attempts to put them into a decipherable order. He continues to look at me with a slightly confused look on his face.

'Actually,' I mutter, 'you are exactly who I was expecting. I worked it all out.' It feels as though the blow to my head has dislodged my jaw, and the bone languishing against bone sends waves of pain down the left side of my face. I poke my tongue around my mouth to check for damage. One of my teeth near the back has definitely been chipped.

Richard smiles down at me with a look of disbelief on his face. 'Well, aren't you a smart little cookie? I thought I might've tricked you when Jack was the one who invited you here—under duress, of course. No one is as tough as they seem with a gun pointed at their head.'

'Where is he?'

'Jack? Oh, he'll be along shortly. So,' he says, pulling up another chair. 'Tell me how you figured out it was me.'

I think carefully how to word it. I can't let slip that it was me, posing as Joseph, that he was talking to on the My Time To Die website.

I move my hand onto my thigh and feel the small lump that tells me Richard has missed the voice recorder in my pocket that has been recording everything since I parked up. With any luck, it will still be recording.

'There were a few things. Firstly, at the hospital…'

'Ah, yes. Untrustworthy Manon. I thought, when you turned up behind me in the queue, that I was done for, there and then. But you seemed to buy my bullshit story about not being allowed access to one of my congregation.'

'I did. For a while, but then I went back to speak to the receptionist and she told me who you were really there to see. Then, I decoded your little prayer book. How very clever of you to use old lady names to mask who you were really talking about. Finally, when I saw the state of Henry's body and the entry of what Henry, or Helena,' Richard smiles at this, 'had done, I put two and two together. Henry killed your wife and child, didn't he?'

'Yes, he did.'

'And you think he deserved to die for that?'

'Yes. But that's not the only reason he died. Do you know he had a daughter?'

I think back to his bedroom and the solitary picture on the set of drawers of a little girl.

'And did you know that he was an abusive father?'

I shake my head.

'Well, he was. He told Jack himself. He hated himself for it and was trying to get help to deal with his anger. An abusive parent definitely deserves to die.'

'So you beat him to death?'

'With my bare hands. Or rather, gloved hands. I'm not stupid enough to leave my fingerprints all over a corpse. And you know something? It felt great.'

Through the grogginess, Liam's handwritten sheet swims into my mind.

'You killed your father. Your biological father, didn't you?'

'Technically, *I* didn't. But if you offer enough money to someone, they'll do anything. I paid a man to kill my father and his friend, so that it would look gang related. I liked the remoteness of it. My alcoholic excuse for a father was dead because of me, but I didn't have to get my hands dirty. What I didn't like was the paper trail.'

I'm almost about to mention My Time To Die, before remembering that, at the minute, he doesn't know that I know about it.

'But why kill the others? What did they do to you?' I ask instead.

He laughs at this. A hollow laugh that echoes around the empty room.

'They are all a scourge on society. They fill the streets with drugs, they beat each other up, they compete to see who can cause the most devastation. My wife and child dying in a crash, that that fucker didn't even stop for, is only the tip of the iceberg. I was—I am—doing a service, ridding the streets of human waste.'

'Doesn't the Bible teach you to love thy neighbour?' I ask, and again he laughs.

'Oh, it says plenty, but I stopped believing that shit the moment my wife and baby were killed. No fair God would let that happen. The world is built on chaos, and as they say, if you can't beat them, join them.'

'So why didn't you kill them yourself? Why prey on the vulnerable, the ones that you should be helping? Why get suicidal people to murder, before they kill themselves, on your instruction?'

'I thought, and this is genuine,' he says, holding two hands up, 'that I was helping them. I was giving them a way out of a life that they didn't want to live anymore. I was a guiding light in a world of darkness. I know how they felt.'

'You don't feel shit,' I shout.

'I do, believe me, I do. I know exactly how they feel. My father abused me as a child and my mother did nothing to stop it. That's why I killed him. I swore revenge on him, and revenge on a world that didn't care about me.' He stands up. 'But, actually, all I wanted to do was end it all. No one would've cared. My parents certainly wouldn't have. But I was more scared of dying than of living. So, I fought through it. I was a nightmare for many years. I was a drug addict and an alcoholic. I got myself into all sorts of nastiness. But I found God and changed my life. I got clean, I trained as a priest and promised to myself that I would be a force for good.'

I give a snort of derision.

'For many years, I was. But there is only so much one man can take.'

'So what's next?' I ask.

'Well, in the immediate future, someone who needed my guidance in leaving this world behind, is coming here to end his life and yours.'

I pretend to act shocked and ham up the sadness in my voice. 'Why me?'

'Because you are the one who ended this all for me. There is no way I can carry on with my cleansing, as I believe you will have shared your intel with your colleagues. I believed, and still do believe, that what I have done is the right thing.'

He pulls a gun from his waistband and just as he finishes spewing his self-righteous bullshit, there is a knock on the side door. He marches across to it and pulls a set of keys from his pocket. He holds them up to the light and chooses the correct one, inserting it into the lock as another knock reverberates around the church.

When the door is pulled open, my heart performs somersaults at the sight of Andy. They exchange a few words at the door before he is permitted to enter. Whilst he waits for Richard to re-lock the door, he sneaks a glance at me and I nod my head quickly; a sign that we have got what we need. He looks shocked and I realise that I must look like a bloody mess. Richard turns and starts to walk back towards me, gun still in hand. Andy falls into step behind him and I can see him steeling himself for action.

All of a sudden, he lunges at Richard's back, knocking him to the ground. The gun bounces across the floor and I find myself hoping that the safety is on. Andy is on top of Richard, who is face down on the carpet.

The situation seems surreal. Here I am, tied to a chair with blood-matted hair and an open head wound, watching two men grapple on the floor, knowing there is no way to help.

Andy seems in control of the situation, though Richard is trying with all his might to free himself. He manages to get an arm free and throws the long limb back, catching Andy in the nose with his elbow. Andy falls backwards, blood squirting immediately from both nostrils, relinquishing the upper hand in the struggle. At the same time as the blow landed on Andy's nose, the door to the office burst open and a bloodied and battered Jack stumbles out of it. He takes a moment to take in what is happening, before lunging for the gun at the same time as Richard. Both of their hands edge towards the weapon, but Andy manages to get hold of Richard's leg, halting his momentum. Jack picks up the gun and aims it at Richard's head.

'It's over, asshole,' he says, standing over him, gun trained on the defeated priest. Richard drops his face into the carpet and extends both hands above his head. Andy gets to his feet and cuffs Richard's hands behind his back—the conflict over, both here and on the streets.

Once he is sure that Richard is of no danger, he takes the gun off Jack and makes it safe. Jack takes a step towards Richard's body and aims a kick at his ribs, which connects with a satisfying thud. Richard cries out in agony and Andy pretends not to notice. Jack collapses onto one of the pews, his anger turning to exhaustion. Andy walks over to me and frees me from my restraints.

'Good plan,' he says, with a kind smile, though his teeth are stained with his own blood. 'Now, let's get you to hospital.'

29

I WINCE AS the doctor finishes stitching the gash in my head back together. He's pretty sure I have a concussion and orders me to stay put, though I tell him I have someone to see. He says he will turn a blind eye for ten minutes, but when he comes back, I'd best be here.

I follow him out of the door and walk to the room currently housing Richard. Andy is sitting outside and a uniformed officer guards the door.

'Have you been in yet?' I ask, making Andy jump.

He gets out of his seat and hugs me. 'How are you feeling?'

'Like I've been bashed over the head with a baseball bat,' I reply, and he laughs.

He releases me. 'Looks nasty,' he says, examining the top of my head. 'How many stitches?'

'Ten.'

For the first time since the church, I'm able to take him in. His nose looks a little off centre and his T-shirt is stained with his own blood. 'Sorry about your nose,' I say. 'That wasn't part of the plan.'

'Don't be silly,' he smiles, 'I let him do it. I've always wanted a crooked nose. Shows character. That's the only reason I play rugby. I'm assuming him smashing you over the head with the butt of a gun also wasn't part of the plan?'

'I thought he'd try and drug me. That seemed to be his usual go-to.'

'Well, in that case, you must've really pissed him off with all your meddling.'

We both laugh, though the outcome of the night could've been so much different. As it is, a concussion and a broken nose are small prices to pay to take another psychopath off the streets.

'Have you seen Jack?' I ask.

Andy nods. 'Yeah, he's getting patched up. Luckily, Richard went pretty light on him. He got him to ring you under threat of being shot, and when that was done, he smacked him around a bit and tied him to a chair.'

'He loves tying people to chairs, doesn't he?'

'It certainly seems to be his thing. Anyway, Jack managed to get a set of keys from the desk and cut through the rope that was holding him.'

'With impeccable timing.'

Andy nods in agreement.

'Shall we?' he asks.

The officer stands to the side and allows us to enter the room. Inside, Richard sits, his wrists handcuffed to the metal arms of the chair. Another officer sits in the corner of the room, keeping an eye on him.

'So, you found out about my site?' he says. 'Well played, Joseph.'

'Why?' I ask simply.

'Well, I told you everything in the church. I wanted to clean up the streets, but I didn't want to get my hands dirty. I also told you that when I arranged for my father's death, I didn't like the fact that the man I paid money to kill him could turn me in on a whim. I was reckless, then. Not now. So, I set up this site for two reasons. Firstly, to genuinely help people end their lives. Secondly, to get those people to do my bidding.'

'How did you choose who to bring in?'

'Firstly, by location. That's why I asked for region on sign up. I knew that if someone travelled from Edinburgh or London, it might raise more suspicion. Best to keep it local. I let the attention seekers chat amongst themselves and targeted those that meant it. You can tell by the language they use. Many of those who I targeted were repulsed by the idea. They simply wanted to end their own life and were not interested in taking another with them. Because everything is faceless, it didn't matter. I got on with my day and they got on with theirs. Luckily, there were three who did what I needed them to do. Well, two,' he says through gritted teeth. 'Not that French bitch. The way to do it is to dangle the carrot of help in front of them and then take it away when they resist. Tell them you will provide a gun for them to use, but only as long as they use it on someone else too. If they refuse, you move that gun an inch out of the picture and the truly fucked up ones quickly realign themselves with my way of thinking.'

'Why did you take to Joseph so quickly?' I ask.

He laughs. 'By that stage, you were getting close to uncovering everything, and I needed you gone. It was a lapse in judgement to trust him so quickly. And look where it has got me.'

I've heard enough.

'Richard Clark, you are under arrest for the murders of Marcus Sharpe, Clive Burston, Kai McCormick, Zoe Sullivan, Charlie Hill and Henry Mayfield. Also, for the attempted murder of Manon Marchand and myself, Erika Piper. You do not have to say anything, but it may harm your defence if you do not mention, when questioned, something which you later rely on in court.'

He simply bows his head and remains silent, so Andy and I leave him in the capable hands of the officer in the room.

We walk back to my room. I'm keen to stay on the doctor's good side, given that he is in charge of my painkillers. I sit down on the bed and Andy takes a chair.

'Thanks for tonight, Andy,' I say. 'If it weren't for you…'

'Don't mention it, partner. Maybe, as a thank you, you could start calling me Ro…'

'I am not calling you Robbo,' I laugh.

Just then, the door bursts open and Tom comes storming in, followed by DCI Bob.

'What the fuck do you think you're playing at?' Tom shouts.

Andy stands up and gives me an awkward nod, before squeezing past a raging Tom and out the door. So much for our partnership!

'I didn't think he was going to hit me,' is all I manage before he envelopes me in the tightest hug I've ever been given. He is still hugging me when DCI Bob speaks.

'What a force of nature you are. Well done for tonight.'

Tom looks annoyed that I'm being congratulated for putting my life on the line.

'Remember,' he says, his voice clipped. 'It's not just your safety that you've got to think about now. We've got the little one on the way.'

'I know,' I interrupt. 'The whole time I was strapped to the chair, it was all I could think about.'

I take a deep breath. Being a police officer is all I have ever wanted to do with my life. I have made so many sacrifices over the years to get to where I am today, to achieve the role of Detective Inspector. But some things are more important than rank or role, and one of those is a child. Especially a child I never thought I'd be lucky enough to have.

'Bob,' I say, 'I'm afraid I'm going to be resigning.'

I was expecting a fight from Bob; or at least for him to ask me to stay. Instead, he looks delighted.

'Thank God for that!' he laughs. 'On the way here, I was brainstorming ways to fire you.'

He sits down on the chair opposite me. 'I'm joking, of course. But I think you are making the right decision. If you want, I can try and get you a desk job. That way, you can stay in the job, but you'd be out of the firing line.'

I tell him I'll think about it. He thanks me again for my work tonight, shakes mine and Tom's hand, and leaves.

Alone with Tom, the enormity of the night's events close in on me. I lean my head on his chest and weep. He holds me tight, strokes my hair and makes soothing noises and I am quickly filled with the beautiful feeling that Tom is going to make an excellent father.

30

A SLIVER OF silvery moon rests high in the dark November night sky as Andy, his wife Marie, Tom and I leave the pub.

'How's the desk job?' Andy asks, his eyes unfocussed and his speech slightly slurred.

His wife slaps him on the shoulder. 'She's already told you about it twice tonight.'

'Oh, right,' he laughs, but doesn't follow up for fear of another slap. 'I can't believe we were only partners for a month. Am I really that bad?'

Everyone laughs and Tom slips his arm around my waist and pulls me close. His other hand rubs the front of my slightly rounded stomach.

'I made her quit,' Tom says. 'I couldn't let her be partnered with a Liverpool fan.' Andy gives him the middle finger in return.

'It's our year, I reckon,' he replies. 'Unless something catastrophic happens.'

We walk as a foursome down the street towards our houses. Andy tells us about some of the ongoing cases and about the new Detective Chief Inspector, now that Bob has gone. He has had a little too much to drink, and his Scottish-Scouse hybrid has become even harder to understand.

We bid them goodbye when they get to their cul-de-sac before continuing our journey home. Whilst I'm waiting for Tom to unlock the door, I feel a thump in my stomach that shocks me. I realise that the baby has kicked for the first time and squeal excitedly for Tom to rest his hand on my tummy. I look to the sky, smiling, as the baby performs some sort of breakdance within me, and mentally share my exciting news with Liam, the godfather in the stars.

21st February 2020

I LOOK AT the nurse standing beside my bed through groggy eyes.

'Sorry to wake you,' she says, 'but it's time for your tablets.'

With some effort, I shuffle as far as I can into a seated position, and take the little plastic cup containing the tablets from her. I pop them in my mouth and gulp them down with some cold water, like a seasoned pro. She takes the cup from me, pops it in the bin and moves to the end of my bed, taking the clipboard in her hands and poring over my notes.

'A bit of a bumpy birth, then,' she says, looking up.

'It hurt like fuck,' I reply, and her face falls slightly before breaking into a wide smile.

'It does tend to,' she laughs. She looks over at a grinning Tom, who is sitting beside my bed, cuddling a wad of blankets like they are the most precious thing on Earth. Which, of course, they are. He moves the bundle slightly to show the contents to the nurse.

The only thing visible is a tiny face. Thin red lines mark the areas where the midwife had to use forceps to pull the baby from its cosy home into the big, wide world. A tiny tongue protrudes from between ruby lips, excited by the prospect of some milky goodness.

The sight of my little bundle of joy, coupled with the hormones flooding my body, causes tears to spill down my face. Happy tears, of course.

'Do you have a name yet?' the nurse asks.

I take a breath.

'Yes. He's called Liam.'

ACKNOWLEDGEMENTS

Thank YOU for reading my book. You will never know how much it means to me that you have spent your time and money on something that has come from my head. It blows my mind and it always will.

There are a number of people I would like to thank...

Everyone at Red Dog Press. They may be a small press, but they are mighty. Sean has worked tirelessly to make this the best it can be—the words, the cover, the physics—everything, and I couldn't be more thrilled with how it has all come out.

To anyone who has taken the time to get in touch with me, to leave a review, to interact in any way. Yes, even you, two-star review man who called A Wash of Black *'twee'*—a woman had her throat slashed for god's sake... Please know that I love hearing from you! Your reaction to A Wash of Black made me feel like a real author and your continued support means the world. I can't wait to hear your thoughts on this one.

To all the authors who took time to provide a quote for me. The moment I saw a photo of MW Craven holding a picture of my book was a ridiculous feeling—a real pinch me moment. I cannot thank you enough for your time and your kind words.

To Adam Carroll, a friend and a wonderful musician. Years ago, in a band called Gunther, he wrote a song called Burning Bridges. The words at the start of the book, from Manon's fictional suicide note, are actually from that song. When I asked if I could use them, he agreed that I could, as long as I sent him a copy of the song. His own song. I'm not sure if me having a copy and him not having one puts me in the mega fan category, but it's where I always hoped I'd end up! Vive el borracho!

To my wife, Sarah, and my beautiful children. My wife continues to inspire me, support me and offer an ear when I lose my way—

even if it is in a detailed description of someone's suffering! Thank you!

Finally, to my Blood Brothers—Sean Coleman and Rob Parker. One of the best things about putting my book out was meeting you two. From the moment I met Rob, at my book launch, I knew we were going to be firm friends. Sean, though technically my boss, is firmly in that camp too. They have been supportive and helpful during this journey. When the opportunity to spend a few hours together, virtually, whilst recording a podcast came about, I leapt at the chance. Time spent with you during this very strange period in the world was a tonic. Thank you, for your friendship.

One last thing. The topic of suicide in this book is one I fretted over for a long time. The lead singer of one of my favourite bands, Frightened Rabbit, committed suicide in 2018. It was a massive deal for me and I didn't know whether it should be considered a taboo subject. The rest of the guys in the band set up a mental health charity in his name—Tiny Changes, with the intention of getting people talking about how they feel. I hope that my treatment of suicide has been sympathetic. I also hope that if you have suffered / are suffering with your mental health, that you know there are people to talk to. Professionals, friends, family, random strangers on twitter who are willing to drop what they are doing to have a chat.

The whole COVID-19 thing has been a minefield for many, but the reading community has been a source of strength for me. Keep talking. Keep making tiny changes.

Lightning Source UK Ltd.
Milton Keynes UK
UKHW011840241120
374027UK00005B/63/J